Published in Nashville, Tennessee by Tommy Nelson™, a division of Thomas Nelson, Inc.

Scripture quotations are from the *International Children's Bible®, New Century Version®:* Copyright © 1986, 1988, 1999 by Tommy Nelson™, a division of Thomas Nelson, Inc.

Creative director: Robin Crouch
Series consultant: Dandi Daley Mackall
Computer programming consultant: Lucinda C. Thurman

Library of Congress Cataloging-in-Publication Data

Smith, Carol, 1961-
    Stranger online / written by Carol Smith ; created by Terry Brown.
        p. cm. – (TodaysGirls.com ; 1)
    Summary: To save her reputation at school and keep her position on the swim team, Amber must uncover the identity of the mysterious stranger who has been sending threatening email messages to her website.
        ISBN 0-8499-7554-9
        [1. Web sites—Fiction. 2. Swimming—Fiction. 3. High schools—Fiction. 4. Schools—Fiction. 5. Christian life—Fiction.] I. Brown, Terry, 1961 – II. Title. III. Series.
    PZ7.S64345 St 2000
    [Fic] – dc21   00-025812
                                                                    CIP

Printed in the United States of America
00 01 02 03 04 05 QWM 0 9 8 7 6 5 4 3 2

STRANGER ONLINE

WRITTEN BY
Carol Smith

CREATED BY
Terry K. Brown

Thomas Nelson, Inc.
Nashville

Web Words

2 to/too

4 for

ACK! disgusted

A/S/L age/sex/location

B4 before

BBL be back later

BBS be back soon

BF boyfriend

BRB be right back

CU see you

Cuz because

CYAL8R see you later

Dunno don't know

Enuf enough

FYI for your information

G2G or GTG I've got to go

GF girlfriend

GR8 great

H&K hug and kiss

IC I see

IN2 into

IRL in real life

JLY Jesus loves you

JK just kidding

JMO just my opinion

K okay

Kewl cool

KOTC kiss on the cheek

LOL laugh out loud

LTNC long time no see

LY love you

L8R later

NBD no big deal

NU new/knew

NW no way

OIC oh, I see

QT cutie

RO rock on

ROFL rolling on floor laughing

RU are you

SOL sooner or later

Splain explain

SWAK sealed with a kiss

SYS see you soon

Thanx (or) thx thanks

TNT till next time

TTFN ta ta for now

TTYL talk to you later

U you

U NO you know

UD you'd (you would)

UR your/you're/you are

WB welcome back

WBS write back soon

WTG way to go

Y why

(Note: Remember that capitalization may vary.)

chapter.1

faithful1: Maybe I should change my user name . . .

Amber pressed *enter*. She had been staring at the screen for hours. In the last part of the conversation still on-screen, only two names were listed in their chat room: her own "faithful1" and her best friend's "nycbutterfly." Maya's user name fit great—she was born in New York City, and she swam the best butterfly on the team.

nycbutterfly: NW!! faithful1!! It's who u r!
faithful1: GR8! But it's boring (like everything else around here) and it's not very cool.
nycbutterfly: Do you want to pretend to be something you're not?

faithful1: So I'm NOT cool?

nycbutterfly: Oops. Didn't mean that the way it
sounded.

faithful1: i know. faithful I am, and faithful1 I'll be.

Amber heard a luscious little sound that meant only one thing: she had new e-mail! She clicked on the mailbox icon, and, in a flash, she could see what somebody had written.

You'll get yours.

There was no address, only a screen name: Stranger.

A chill ran through Amber. Someone, a stranger, had accessed her e-mail while she was in the middle of an upgrade! She leaned back in her chair and tried to think. Who would threaten her? And why? She absently twisted a lock of hair around her finger—a nervous habit she'd had forever.

After a few minutes, while breathing was optional, she shook her head and laughed. It had to be a joke!

Maya never would have sent the e-mail, but Bren could have. She and Bren had been playing tricks on each other since Brownies.

The name chicChick appeared in the chat room roll on the side of Amber's screen.

There she is, thought Amber. *She'll get hers, too.*

chicChick: hi ho, people. What's up?

nycbutterfly: I've just been insulting Amber. What are you into?

chicChick: YOU?? I'm the insulting one . . .

nycbutterfly: not tonight, you're not. Amber wants to change her user name. thinks faithful1's not kewl enuf.

chicChick: whatever. she's had months to think about this . . .

faithful1: yeah, Chic, and you've had months to get me back for taking your naked baby pictures to the cafeteria.

chicChick: what?

faithful1: You feeling strange tonight??

chicChick: What????

faithful1: oh, come on. I'll get mine, Chic? You can't scare me. And you could have dreamed up a better address than "Stranger."

chicChick: ok, what are you blabbering about?

nycbutterfly: ????

faithful1: I just got an e-mail . . . says "you'll get yours." And the sender's address isn't listed. And it's signed "Stranger." I wonder who could've sent it, Bren.

nycbutterfly: EW! Scary. You told us not to give out our e-mail addresses! Or our passwords!!

chicChick. I didn't do it.

faithful1: I must be freaking out. Our site is protected! It's completely secure--who would have known?

chicChick: pinkie promise--it's not me. My sense of humor might be strange, but I'm not your Stranger. When I'm after revenge, I serve it up like Coach says: cold on a silver platter. You won't even suspect me when I get you back for picture day. In fact, I'd forgotten all about that . . .

Amber pulled her eyes away from the screen. *If it's really not them,* she wondered, *then who is it?* She had spent months working on security for TodaysGirls.com. Their site was supposed to be a haven where they could escape the online weirdos in their own private chat room. *I guess I'm not the computer expert I think I am,* she decided.

She had started working on computers before anyone else even had one. Her dad had given her a kiddy-game typing program when she was still in elementary school. And since then, she'd progressed from processing through programming to her current role as computer diva, even at school. She knew their site was impenetrable. So how did the Stranger get her address? Amber glanced back at the screen.

chicChick: r u there, f1?? Hello? Yoo hoo, mission control?

Amber snapped back to reality and typed.

faithful1: sorry. I spaced out for a sec.

nycbutterfly: hey--hit *reply* on his message and see where it takes you.

faithful1: NW. What if it's one of those cyber-freaks like in the public chat rooms?

chicChick: maybe it's just a joke. or a message like one of those fortune cookies that we get down @ Fun Chows?

nycbutterfly: Chic--nobody gets threats in fortune cookies from Fun Chows. I read about a girl who got stalked on the Internet. It's called "cyber-stalking."

Amber's hands hung trembling a half-inch above the keyboard. The word *stalking* threw her off. Her computer suddenly felt alien to her, like a rat had crawled inside and built a nest before she even knew it was there. She leaned over and looked out the window just to see if some weirdo was lurking in the bushes.

"I am freaking out!" she said aloud, forcibly shifting her eyes and fingertips back to the computer screen. Her friends were still debating the e-mail.

chicChick: NYC, you are totally paranoid. It's probably faithful's brother e-mailing her from the den. Go look for Ryan in the den!!!!!

nycbutterfly: I am not paranoid. Maybe it's from Coach--

he could be playing a joke on you.

faithful1: Coach would never do anything creepy like this, and he would never be up this late. My brother's dead meat, too. It's almost midnight.

chicChick: ACK! It IS late. We've got practice in the morning. Go to bed. I'm outta here.

chicChick left the room

nycbutterfly: Amber, seriously, we'd better tell someone about the e-mail tomorrow. But for tonight, you need to chill. This dude, whoever he is, can't crawl through your cables into your room, so it can wait until morning. 'night.

faithful1: thanks, sister. Good night.

Amber printed out the e-mail before she shut everything down for the night. She read it one last time, then she stuffed it in her gym bag with her suit and swim goggles. Morning swim practice waited for no one, and Coach Short was scheduled to pick her up in five short hours.

She brushed her teeth, and then scanned every inch of her face, freckles and all. Mustering a big fake smile, she grinned at herself in the makeup mirror. She could look at Maya and Bren and know that her friends were pretty. Amber squinted her eyes almost shut, making her light freckles disappear altogether, as though she were looking through a frosted lens. Giving up on self-analysis, she scrubbed her face and flipped off the bathroom light.

Sleep didn't come easily for Amber that night. As a kid, she had never been scared of monsters under the bed. Or in the closet. But the image of something crawling through her computer cables like a virus in her bloodstream kept returning. She sat up and looked around her room. There was enough light through the blinds so she could make out familiar shapes like her computer table, her big stuffed dog from last year's fair, and the coat tree in the corner. She could see the green numbers on the stereo clock peeking through the half-open door of her antique wardrobe as if they were blinking sleepily at her.

She flounced back on her pillow. *What am I doing? I'm in my own bedroom. The Stranger can just take a hike.* Still, after a few more sleepless tosses, she turned on the table lamp, walked over to her desk, and unplugged her computer and its phone line. *It can't hurt,* she thought, *but I'll never tell anyone that I did this.*

Amber's alarm clock shrieked its unwelcome cry, urging her awake from across the room. A muffled "thud" against the wall let her know that she'd woken up her brother as well.

"Turn that stupid clock off!" Ryan yelled through the wall.

Amber ignored him. She hunkered deeper under her down comforter, pulling her pillow over her head. If he didn't care enough to get out of bed, he must not be that bothered. And this reasoning held out until Ryan's voice boomed next to her ear.

"I SAID TURN THAT STUPID MUSIC OFF!"

"Get over it," Amber snarled, swooping up and stomping

across the room to turn off the radio. She sounded tough, but she was putting as much distance between herself and Ryan as she could manage.

Ryan's eyes were barely open. His hair looked like someone had pulled it up into several ponytails when it was wet and left it overnight before setting it free. He still had a glob of acne cream on his chin and sleep dust in his eyes.

"If the girls could see you now," Amber teased, "they wouldn't be chasing you, big brother."

"I don't care if you and your stupid friends like to get up in the middle of the night. But the rest of us don't want to wake up with you!" he bellowed, turning sharply and retreating toward his dark, messy cave of a room. He slammed his door.

Amber had to smile. She wasn't bothering *the rest of them.* Her parents' bedroom was at the other end of the house. She was just bothering Ryan. The truth was she enjoyed it . . . except when he sneaked up on her. She slammed her own door shut just to make a point, and then she spotted headlights shining through her window.

Amber knew exactly what would happen next, so she took her time gathering her books and stuffing a pair of towels in her bag. Coach would send Morgan to ring the doorbell. He had no patience. Amber could've run to catch Morgan before she rang, but since the doorbell speaker was right beside Ryan's door . . . *Ding-dong, Ding-dong* . . . She just let it ring as she dashed down the hallway, smiling at her brother's muffled wails.

"Amber!" he yelled. "If he blows that stupid horn one more time . . . I'm going to get you!"

I'm going to get you. You'll get yours. The front doorknob turned to ice and froze Amber's arm halfway up. Instantly the October air felt ten degrees colder.

chapter.2

Coach Short popped the back hatch as Amber walked to the van. She threw in her stuff and then checked her watch by the door light hovering above her head. It was 5:05. He wasn't supposed to pick her up until 5:15!

"Hey! Why so early?" she asked, rearranging the identical gym bags into a single layer. "I should've made you wait another ten minutes."

"Come on, Amber," Coach grumbled. "We'll start practice on time for once. The chauffeur gets to have his way sometimes."

Amber walked around to the front of the van and found Alex Diaz riding shotgun. *What is the new kid doing in my seat again?* she wondered. Amber always sat up front, even when she was picked up last. She wasted a dirty look on Alex as she climbed through the sliding side door. She bent over to scrunch past

11

Morgan in the middle seat and had a nice surprise. "Bren, what are you doing here?" she cried. Even though Bren was officially on the team, she rarely showed up.

"And good morning to you, too," Bren said, smiling from her window seat.

"Seriously, what's up?" Amber asked as she plopped in behind her. "You never swim in the morning!"

"Hey!" Bren laughed. "Afraid I might show you up, Backstroke Queen?"

"Do you still know how to swim?" Amber asked sarcastically.

"That was harsh," Bren answered with a smirk. "If you must know, Coach asked me to personally help you all get ready for Tuesday night's meet." Even if Bren's swimming skills were lacking, she never lacked enthusiasm for her teammates.

"Cool," said Amber. "So are you gonna get wet? Trash your pretty hair and perfect makeup like the rest of us?"

"I resent that," Bren hissed, pretending to ignore Amber by peering out the window. The street lamps lit Bren's grinning face intermittently.

Bren really did care about her appearance. She babied her smooth, creamy tan skin. And she always wore her thick, dark brown hair in the latest fashion: for now, it was straight and cut just above her shoulders. The street lights lit up her brown eyes like they had little white Christmas lights blinking inside them.

"Actually," Amber continued, "it's nice to see a new face at this wretched hour, particularly one as perfect as yours."

"Gag me, gag me!" said Alex from the front, turning around in her seat . . . in Amber's seat. "Please, can we talk about something besides makeup and hair this morning?"

Alex's idea of makeup was the tube of lip balm in her pocket. She was pretty in her own way, with her long, natural curls, but looks were not her priority.

"How about boys?" offered Morgan, tossing a crispy M&M into the air, catching it in her mouth. "Boys are a good topic, don't you think?" When the peace required a keeper, Morgan always stepped in. She was a pretty girl, but she was more interested in making other people happy than in drawing attention to herself. If Morgan were stranded in a lifeboat after a shipwreck, she'd be the one making sure everyone's life jacket was buckled.

"Let's talk about who sits where in the van," Amber suggested sweetly. Alex kept her head turned toward the window, saying nothing.

Although Amber still simmered about Alex snagging her favorite seat, she felt the familiar relief about being last in line for pickup. Amber lived in Coach's neighborhood, but as a favor to her, he picked up the other girls and then circled back by her house. This time of year, by the time the van arrived, it was all warm inside, and most of the whiners had aired their morning complaints.

Amber and Coach Short had talked about it a million times. Who could blame the team for complaining a little? Who in their right mind would want to get up in the pitch-black, cold night and head to a swimming pool? Who?

Coach Harrison Short, that's who! He thought that picking them up was the only way to be sure swim practice started on time. It reminded Amber of those newscasters on the morning shows who got picked up in limousines just so they wouldn't be late. But Coach really did care about his team members. He even liked them. Amber knew that she wasn't the only one who felt favored—each girl felt like she was Coach's individual pride and joy. He could be gruff, but Amber was glad she got to ride with him—she just didn't enjoy the time of day.

And she didn't enjoy Alex's acting like all that when she had only been around since August. Everybody knew the upper-classmen got dibs on the best stuff. At least when Amber was a freshman, the upperclassmen sure did. They got the front seats in the van and on the buses. They got the showers first. And they never had to do grunt work for Coach, like putting out lane markers or sweeping the area. As far as Amber was concerned, Alex was one freshman who was way out of line. She didn't look too sad about it, either, and that made Amber resent her even more.

"Hey, Morgan," Amber cried, suddenly noticing Maya's absence. "Where's your big sister? Is she sick?"

"Dad got Maya's old VW out of the shop yesterday—again—so she drove to school early," Morgan answered, turning around. "Jamie was going to ride with her and practice driving in the school parking lot. If it keeps running. Dad calls that car a classic, but it's just old."

"I'm amazed you rode with us," Bren said, feigning surprise. "This lacks the same sense of adventure as a Jamie cruise, even if it's just around the lot."

Morgan smiled at Bren. "I just wanted to know I would get to school in one piece. Have you ever seen Jamie driving a stick shift? She makes the car bounce up and down. Really. Like a basketball. I don't know how Maya stands it."

"So that's what the back brace in the backseat is all about," Bren said as if she were solving a mystery.

Morgan laughed aloud. "Between Jamie's driving and that beater of a car, I figure Coach is a better bet."

"Oh, now I like that," Coach Short chimed in. "I'm no adventure, but at least I'm dependable, huh?"

"Coach," Bren added, "you at five o'clock in the morning is like an alarm that rings ugly and has no snooze." As Bren was making her jab, she threw her stuff into the backseat, then threw herself over the seat as well.

Morgan, Coach, and Alex debated the merits of an ugly alarm while Bren started questioning Amber. "So, did you figure out who sent the weird e-mail?"

"No, and sh-h-h-h!" whispered Amber. "I don't want the whole world to know."

"I'm being quiet," Bren muttered. "And besides, Coach is distracting the munchkins."

"It's not Morgan and Alex I'm worried about," Amber explained. "I don't want hound dog Harrison Short to start sniffing this trail. You know how overprotective he gets. Besides, I think I know who sent it." Amber hadn't stopped thinking about the Stranger, and one name kept coming back to her mind—Jake Smith. She and Jake had known each other forever. Their parents were still close friends, but Jake had turned kind of weird since they hit high school.

"You're kidding!" Bren whispered. "Who? You don't have any enemies, do you?"

"I don't think it's an enemy," Amber replied. "I think it's someone who wants something from me." That *something* was letting Jake copy off her paper in chemistry lab.

"Like sending threatening e-mail would be the way to get anything from anybody. Who would do it—hack into our Web site, figure out just your e-mail address, and then threaten you anonymously? 'You'll get yours.' Amber, tell me! Who do you think it is?"

Amber wanted to tell her. But she didn't want to get Jake into trouble. He already had enough of that. "Drop it, Bren," Amber whispered. "If it's who I think it is, there's nothing to worry about. He's harmless. Just a pest."

"What if it's not your harmless pest?" Bren whispered back. "What if it's someone really dangerous? Don't you think we should tell Coach? Or your mom?"

"I can handle it," Amber said just a little too loud.

"You can handle what, Amber?" asked Coach Short. The tone was light, but in the rearview mirror she could see his eyebrows rising, wrinkling across his forehead. She didn't like to worry him, but if he nosed in now, she'd never keep the e-mail a secret until she could make sure she was right about Jake.

Bren tried for a save: "You know Amber. She doesn't want anyone to know she flosses twice a day. She's into privacy."

Bren's cover only raised the curiosity of the coach. He tried again: "Really, Amber, is something going on I should know about? And you know I should know about anything that's going on."

Just then a beige sports car ran a stop sign and drove directly into the van's path. Coach swerved as the girls grabbed ceiling handles and seats in front of them to steady themselves.

The van stopped, then surged ahead again as Amber reeled mentally through a list of subjects she could use to redirect the conversation. She could ask him about his boys. Too obvious. Or his yard—his favorite obsession. That wouldn't work, not this time of year. She settled on the upcoming swim meet as a topic. Everyone could grab onto that and chew for a while.

By the time Coach had finished informing the sports car driver where she ranked on the idiot meter, Amber was ready to launch her strategic alternate-conversation plan.

"Hey! I am so pumped about Tuesday's meet," she said enthusiastically, "Are you all ready?"

"Texans are born ready!" Alex chimed in, and Amber's plan

swung into success. "Back home I took the state freestyle record for the past two years."

"What?" sputtered Bren. "Oh, come on, Alex. You were in junior high! You don't think you're going to break Indiana records on a winning team when you're just a freshman, do you?"

"All I'm saying is . . ." Alex hesitated, probably trying to think of what she was saying.

Morgan, as usual, came to her rescue, ". . . is that a winning attitude is everything. You won't be upperclassmen forever, you know. This team is ours eventually, and we might as well think like winners now."

"Right!" said Alex.

"You tell 'em Morgan!" cheered Coach Short.

"I'm going to be so sick. Now," pleaded Bren.

Feeling kind of sick myself, thought Amber. What am I going to do about the Stranger?

The van bounced down the school driveway over four abrupt speed bumps that boomeranged each of the girls off their seats. The rest of the team waited by the gymnasium doors— that is, everyone except Maya and Jamie. They were in the middle of the parking lot, crouched over the hood of the VW like they knew what to do next. As the van bobbed past them, Coach yelled, "What's up?"

"It's dead!" Maya yelled back.

"Again! Will you help us, Harry?" Jamie added.

He waved for them to come inside. Amber knew Coach

would help them with the car later, just as he always did when Jamie asked. But for now, it was time to swim. He screeched to a stop, parking across three spaces.

The chilly air hit them with an impact, taking their breath away. The swimmers walked close together, as Coach loped around back to let them in. Amber could hear Alex drilling Morgan.

"Why is the coach always taking care of stuff for Jamie? Are they related or something?"

"They aren't related," Morgan answered, "but he's sort of like a dad to her. He helps Jamie out with stuff her mom doesn't know how to do. Some things are just 'dad' things. You should know, since your parents are still back in Texas."

"Yeah, I guess. My grandpa usually takes care of that stuff here. When I go back home, though, then my dad will do it again." Alex's voice faded off. She looked at her teammates with a weak smile.

Amber somehow knew that Alex's dad didn't always do the "dad" things. And she also knew Alex wasn't going back home anytime soon. Until Alex was ready, though, no one would say it out loud. But Morgan was the only one to smile back at Alex, sealing some kind of silent pact between them.

They walked up to the gym doors just as Coach clanged them open, bellowing his familiar call. "Time to swim! Time to swim! Grab your stuff and come on in."

"Not again!" Amber complained as she clawed through the

gym bag. "Who picked up my bag?" She stormed around the locker room, looking for a familiar head of long russet hair. *I might have known. Alex did it again.*

chapter.3

By the time Amber found Alex, Alex was holding up the bag in her hands as an offering. "I'm sorry, Amber. I must have grabbed your bag by mistake. Sorry."

"Maybe it was a mistake, Alex, but this is happening way too much. It's like a bad habit that you need to break. Take the time to look at the name tag. Our bags might look alike, but our names sure don't."

Amber grabbed her bag and rushed to get suited up for practice. She didn't usually blow her cool so easily. But Alex had made the same mistake with the gym bag at least twice before. Worst of all, the Stranger's e-mail was stuffed in the bag. The last thing Amber needed was a mouthy freshman getting access to something like that.

By the time Amber headed out to the pool, the other girls

had gathered by the bulletin board while Coach made announcements.

"OK, girls, this is Friday. If our next meet is Tuesday night, then how many practices do we have left after today?"

"Three," the group groaned together.

Coach clapped his hands loudly together. "Right! That means that we've got to stay focused and organized. I've posted the lineup on the bulletin board. If you have questions about the events, check there first and then ask me.

"I shouldn't have to remind you how important these invitationals are. You'll be swimming against some of the best teams in our district. If we each set a goal of beating our own best times, then we're sure to come out of the water as winners. Now, let's warm up."

In the water, Amber forcibly pushed her mind past fears of strangers and stalkers, straining her muscles to strengthen each stroke farther than the one before. Oblivious to the other swimmers around her, she felt the familiar release of tension that always came during practice. Usually in practice, you can't beat your best time. But if you're pumped and swimming with great concentration, you might be able to.

Amber moved through the water, head slightly tilted up, creating a wave around her body. Almost automatically, her body swayed from side to side as each arm reached for the water, slightly rubbing against her ear as the pinky finger entered first. Fingers together, hands slightly cupped, she pulled herself through the water. When she concentrated, Amber could hear nothing but the water rushing past and the sharp splash when each hand hit the surface.

"0.58.9!" Coach shouted. "You broke your best by .10, Amber!"

Amber came out of the pool feeling like she could single-handedly face anything.

All of the girls outdid themselves for a Friday. Maya's butterfly was the smoothest it had been all week. And Morgan's time in the breaststroke even made Coach Short smile at the stopwatch. While Amber hated to admit it, Alex Diaz could easily give any competitor a panic attack in freestyle. Personality issues aside, they were a relay team to be reckoned with.

As Amber headed toward the locker room, she thought, *If Alex could just be as easy to get along with as she was to swim with, then life would be a lot better.* She whispered a silent prayer to God under her breath: "Please give me the patience to deal with her," she asked. "I'm gonna need a whole bucket of it today. Amen."

The locker room was lined with sinks on one side and mirrors with counters and outlets on the other. By the lockers were a couple of hand dryers that blew hot air, placed high on the wall so that if all the outlets were being used, they could serve as last resort blow-dryers. But so far from the mirrors, their users were mostly freshmen.

With only two private shower stalls, Amber and Maya were

always the first to hit the showers. They had their routine down so well that they could get from the pool to their first class within twenty minutes—that's if no one got in their way. Important on days like today, when Amber knew Mr. Kistler had a quiz waiting in first block. If she rushed, Amber knew she'd have time to look over her reading from the night before.

Towel-drying her hair, Amber could hear Alex's angry voice sifting through the shower curtain. She listened closely.

"The upperclassmen storm into the showers like we don't even matter at all," Alex said. "They get first dibs on everything, and I'm tired of it. Don't you get tired of it, Morgan?"

"I don't really think about it, Alex," Morgan's voiced cooed. "I just know when I'm the upperclassman, I want the same privileges they have. If you try to fight seniority, you're just going to make more enemies than friends. Amber's the oldest, so she gets first choice, then Maya and on down. You and I are still at the bottom of the list for now."

"So what if it's always been that way?" asked Alex. "And so what that Amber is the oldest? I can beat her at swimming, and I can beat her at this little game, too. You watch. I'm going to get to my first class with dry hair for once."

Amber wrapped her head in one towel and knotted the other one around her like a sarong. She half-smiled at Bren, who rolled her eyes as she waited outside the shower stall. Amber padded into the locker room, remembering to exercise the patience she'd prayed for.

Alex had disappeared from the locker room, but Jamie was sprawled on her back across one of the long benches. Jamie had on her White Sox baseball cap, even though she'd have to take it off before her first class. It was her trademark, like part of her personal uniform. Her thin, straight blonde hair was hanging in a ponytail stuffed through her hat's back strap.

Jamie held a magazine above her face and began reading loudly enough to include the whole team. 'How to know when a guy really likes you,' she announced.

"Oh, no," Maya groaned, throwing her wet things on the bench opposite Jamie.

"Shhhhh," Jamie urged. 'Number one: When you're in the same social scene as your favorite guy, does he talk: (1) only to you, (2) only to *his* friends, (3) only to *your* friends, or (4) only to *himself?*'"

"Jamie, it does not say that." Amber laughed, whipping her towel off her head and cracking it like a whip at Jamie's magazine. Morgan caught the end of the towel from the other side of the bench, launching a tug-of-war match above Jamie, who squealed appropriately as her friends' wet hair showered her with water.

Alex marched in, already changed into her clothes, and headed straight to the mirrors. She unplugged Amber's hair dryer, pushed Maya's makeup out of the way, and plugged in her own blow-dryer. As she blew her long hair back, the rest of the team simply stared at her in dull amazement. Amber couldn't move.

"Why are you looking at me like that?" Alex asked, catching sight of their faces in the mirror.

Jamie walked over to the outlet, unplugged Alex's hair dryer, and plugged Amber's dryer back into the wall beside the mirror.

"Aren't you even going to take a shower?" Jamie asked.

"I don't have to take two showers every morning," Alex protested, unplugging Amber's dryer again to plug in her own again. "I just got out of the pool. And I don't have time to wait for slowpokes to get ready. Go back to your little quiz about landing your man, and let me get ready for class."

Morgan was the only one who seemed capable of action. She grabbed Alex's wet neon-green bathing suit and threw it at her. She then picked up her own suit, took Alex by the arm, and marched her into the junk room.

Amber couldn't stand it. She opened the junk room door to follow them, then changed her mind. Morgan had already turned on the light, so Amber settled in behind the door, where she could peek through the crack. Broken lane markers and pool cleaning nets dangled from the walls. Some old desks formed a circle in the center of the small room. An old refrigerator hummed from the corner, its sole contents Coach's lunch and two bags of ice for first aid.

Morgan was hanging up her hot-pink suit. "Alex," she said, "you'd better loosen up about Amber. She hasn't done anything to you. When you're a junior, aren't you going to want the privileges attached to it?"

"I'm not even going to be in Edgewood when I'm a sophomore," Alex answered, throwing her own suit over the rack. "I'm just sick of Amber. Everybody treats her like she's perfect, and I can't stand it. Every time I think about her I get mad."

Every time she thinks about me, she gets mad? Amber stepped away from the door, plugged her dryer back in, and checked out her friends—her real friends.

Jamie had resumed her sprawl across the bench. Bren and Maya stopped whispering and glanced over at Amber.

"Everything okay?" Maya asked.

"Every time I think about *her* I get mad," Amber said to no one in particular in the locker room. "That's not totally true—but every time I think about Alex, I do have to pray so I *won't* get mad."

Amber bent at the waist and started drying her hair upside down. "Who does she think she is?" she continued. "First, she takes my seat in the van and then moves all my stuff in the locker room. Is this girl from another planet or what?"

"I know," Bren answered. "It's like she's never heard of seniority. It's like she never learned the rules. Hey, maybe we ought to teach her a little lesson about the way things work. What do you think, Amber? It's our responsibility as role models."

Maya piped in, "Bren and I'll watch for her. Amber, you do the deed."

Amber stood up, turning off her dryer and smiling at her friends. "Somebody sure taught us when we were freshmen. Maybe this will straighten her out."

For the most part, Amber tried not to talk bad about anyone. She tried to keep to herself and solve her own problems and let everyone else solve theirs. But she was relieved that her girlfriends had come up with a plan for Alex. Especially a harmless plan.

Harmless. Stranger. Wouldn't it be awesome if we could come up with a plan for the Stranger, too?

Morgan and Alex left the junk room together. Morgan threw Amber a weak smile. Amber saw the bond forming between the two freshmen. She also saw how desperately Morgan wanted them to accept her friend. *Good luck, Morgan,* Amber thought. *You've got a hard job ahead of you.*

As soon as the freshmen were out of sight, Maya and Bren stood guard, while Amber snatched Alex's wet neon swimsuit from the line and stuck it in the freezer.

chapter.4

H ey!" Maya yelled. "Wait up!" Amber slowed her pace in the hallway. "What are you gonna do about that e-mail?" she asked, maneuvering through the throng of other students arriving for their first class.

"No clue," Amber answered. "Here," she added, thrusting her hand into her bag and retrieving the printout. "Take a look."

Maya lowered her voice and said, "You know, Amber, this Stranger might be stranger than we think. If he knows your e-mail address before you've even given it out, what else do you think he knows about you?"

They came to a tee in the hallway where they had to either turn right or left. People were packed into the small space. As the girls maneuvered their way to the right side of the crowd, Amber looked up at the black-and-white clock on the wall. How could there be so much to worry about and school hadn't even started for the day? She tried to keep her voice down as she talked to Maya over her shoulder.

"Look, I think I know who sent it, but I can't figure out how in the world he got my address." Once they filtered through the pack, they walked downstairs into the science wing, and the whole world seemed to slow down. The smell of ammonia and formaldehyde wafted into the hallway from the biology lab.

Maya scanned the letter as they turned the corner to Mr. Kistler's chemistry lab. Then she grabbed Amber's arm to slow her to a stop, leaning back against the wall.

"Amber, who? Who is it? Don't make me drag it out of you."

Amber liked to handle things on her own. Even though Maya was her best friend, Amber would prefer not to spill everything. It was obvious, however, that Maya wasn't going to give in this time. Her deep brown eyes were staring lasers into Amber's brain, and she felt Maya's fingertips boring holes in her arm.

"Okay, I give," Amber relented, lowering her voice to a whisper. "I haven't told anybody this, but I think it's Jake Smith."

Maya let go of her best friend's arm and cocked her head to one side as if she didn't hear Amber right. Then, not in anything like a whisper, she asked, "Jake Smith?" When Amber said nothing, Maya repeated his name with a bigger question mark. Before Amber could beg her to be quiet, Maya was almost on the floor in a spasm of laughter. Catching her breath, she said, "That is the last name I was expecting to hear. Isn't he the goofy dude who had an appendicitis attack right in the middle of a pep rally last year? Why and how would Jake Smith write you a threatening anything? He doesn't have the brains to be charming, much less scary."

Surprisingly, Amber felt almost angry at Maya's comments about Jake.

"Maya, he's not a bad person. He's just having a bad time. Jake and I are old friends, and so are our parents. When he was in the hospital last year, I helped him catch up on his schoolwork. Remember last summer, when I got my dad's car stuck in the field across from our house? Jake pulled it out with his Jeep and helped me clean it up before my parents got home. He's not so bad."

Maya looked puzzled. "I remember the car thing, Amber. But if you're so tight with him, why would he threaten you with e-mails he won't even sign?"

"This year Jake is kinda strange, like he's off-line. His dad lost his job, and their whole family is sort of falling apart. Jake used to be so friendly, and now he's always bullying people around. I'm not as sure about him now. He really is a stranger to me, so I thought maybe he was the 'Stranger.'"

Amber moved closer to Maya, looking over each shoulder nervously. "It gets worse. He's been cheating off my papers in chemistry. You know those 'pop' quizzes that Mr. Kistler throws every other day? Jake sits at my lab table. I didn't notice at first, but he's been copying my answers. I tried everything I could think of to get my paper out of his line of sight. But it's impossible at those lab tables. On the last two quizzes, I got so frustrated I just turned them in unfinished. That's why I think he wrote the note."

Maya looked wide-eyed at Amber. "You turned your quiz in unfinished? You sacrificed your grade because some guy is too lazy to study and didn't respect you enough to leave you alone? If that's true, then I think you're the one who's turning into a stranger, Amber."

"It's not that simple, Maya. I don't want to cause hard feelings between Mr. and Mrs. Smith and my parents. Besides, if I go to Mr. Kistler, how do I know he'll believe me? And what will happen to Jake?"

Maya still looked astonished. "Who cares what happens to Jake? You've got to keep up your grade point average, and you can't keep turning in unfinished quizzes. This isn't like you at all. And if he's the Stranger, then he's threatening you, Amber. He's not your friend."

Amber reached out to push the door open. "Look, there's no time to talk about it now. I've got to get in here. I'll figure out how to get Jake off my back. Let's just think of him as offline Jake and save the other problem until later. I can handle it for now."

Amber pushed open the door, but Maya didn't move one

part of her body, least of all her frown. Amber turned back to face her friend again. "The bell is going to ring. Standing in the hall isn't going to solve any of this."

Maya stuffed the e-mail into her back pocket and nodded at Amber. "Maybe not, but we'll see what happens when I find out who wrote this."

What is wrong with me? Amber wondered as she walked to her seat. I've never sidestepped anyone like that. As the bell rang, she could feel her shoulders tensing up.

"Hey! You ready for class?" Jake was all smiles as he slid onto the lab stool across from Amber. He might not be the smartest person in the junior class, but he had a smile that could melt a girl into a puddle. His hair was short and blond with an almost permanent crease around the back. Hat hair.

Amber fought off the urge to smile back at him. "Back off, Jake. It's been a long morning already, and I don't need anybody making it worse." After settling in, Amber asked as nonchalantly as she could, "Jake, what is your e-mail address?"

"E-mail address?" Jake seemed put off by the question. "What makes you think I even have one?"

Amber watched Jake's eyes for signs that he knew what she was hinting at. No matter how deeply she looked, though, she couldn't find any cloak-and-dagger mystery e-mailer. But she couldn't really find the same old Jake either. This Jake was nervous, and his eyes kept looking away. She couldn't be sure he hadn't sent the threat.

Mr. Kistler's voice broke through her thoughts. "Class, please take out a pencil and a piece of paper. We'll have a pop quiz on last night's reading."

Amber heard Jake groan. He whispered, "I didn't get to do the assignment last night. I hate it when he does this." Then she heard him scoot his stool as close as possible to the lab table. She knew why.

"Jake, don't you dare even think about looking at my paper! Get away—"

"Miss Thomas, is there a problem?" Mr. Kistler asked. Jake was looking straight ahead with the look of an innocent fawn, as if he didn't even know Amber.

"No, sir, just getting ready for the quiz," she answered quietly.

"All right then. Let's begin. Answer the ten questions on the board, please."

The chemical formula for sodium dichromate, Amber thought, *is $Na_2Cr_2O_7 \cdot 2H_2O$. Ha! This is cake . . .*

But as she worked through the next five questions, Amber struggled to block Jake's view. Somehow, he found a way to wait until she had started on the next question, and then he copied her answer to the question before. Amber knew that if their answers were too alike, Mr. Kistler would never believe that she hadn't let Jake cheat. She also had a good idea why Jake hadn't done his homework. He was probably taking care of his dad. It seemed like every time she saw Mr. Smith anymore, he was on the couch looking as if he had eaten bad food. Jake was always taking care of stuff around the house. She wanted to help him, but this didn't seem like the best way.

There was something else that bothered Amber about the whole deal. What about her own sense of right and wrong? It was important to her to do what was right. The problem was that it was hard to please God and please everyone else at the same time. Even though she knew it wasn't true, God seemed somehow farther away than Jake, who was breathing over her left arm, or Mr. Kistler, who was shuffling papers instead of making sure nobody copied.

Finally, at question six Amber just turned over her paper. She couldn't keep Jake from cheating, so she wouldn't give him any more answers to steal. Her GPA was high enough that she could sacrifice a few points. She heard Jake beside her writing. *He doesn't mean to be mean,* she thought. *But he's messing us both up, and nobody else knows about this little war we're both losing.*

chapter.5

"So we mix the orange stuff with the water, and you write down what happens, right?" Jake asked.

Amber knew it really wasn't a question. It was his way of getting out of work.

She glanced at Jake before she answered, thinking through her best attack. She started measuring the crystalline salt and decided to use reason rather than guilt.

"Jake, you know you can do this work. This isn't an honors class. So why are you always trying to get someone else to do your work for you?"

"Oh, so what's a little sharing answers? And what's with not finishing your quiz? You know being so uptight is going to cost us both a grade or two."

Amber handed Jake an empty beaker and put on her most

patient voice. "Your grades are not my responsibility, Jake. I helped you out last year, but I didn't do your work for you. You need to get off my back and start taking care of yourself."

Jake slammed down the beaker, and the whole class jumped. "Sorry," he said to the class. Then in a whisper that chilled her, he said to Amber, "Look, I've got about more pressure than I can stand. You can help me, or you can get in my way. It's your choice."

Amber poured water into the beaker, added the sodium dichromate, and reached for her pencil. "It's not that I don't want to help you, Jake. But helping you and cheating on a test are two different things."

"Oh yeah? Well let me tell you something, Amber. You think you're so holy, so high and mighty. But one of these days, you are going to need help from somebody. When you do, you'll find out what it's like when somebody says no in your face just like you're doing in mine. You'll get what you deserve."

Amber held her breath. *You'll get what you deserve.* It sounded way too close to *you'll get yours.* The e-mail was now in Maya's pocket.

Jake snapped his fingers in front of Amber's entranced face. "Oh good grief, Amber. Just write down the reaction time." Then in his best TV narrator voice he said, "Nobody cheated while making this experiment." He waited for a laugh from Amber. When he didn't get one, he added, "Let's finish up and get out of here. Class is almost over. Mr. Kistler is starting to dust his desk. That means he's ready to go."

Amber joined the rush to get out of chemistry class, but Mr. Kistler stopped her as she passed his desk. "Amber, I need to talk with you."

Amber felt as guilty as if she'd been the one cheating. "Me?"

"I've asked Coach Short if we could meet in his office." Mr. Kistler scooped his notebooks under one arm and led the way.

As she silently trailed after him, Amber imagined prison bars lining the halls. The other prisoners did double takes to see who was being led down death row.

"Harry!" Kistler called, as soon as they entered the pool area. "Are you in here?"

"Of course I'm in here, Frank," Coach Short called from his office. "Come on in."

Amber followed Kistler into Coach's office. She glanced around the pool to make sure nobody was there. Somehow, she knew this wasn't going to be pretty.

"We've got a problem with your star in the backstroke category, Harry," said Mr. Kistler, taking the only empty chair in the office and leaving Amber to stand there like a coatrack, which probably would have been safer.

"Amber? What kind of problem could you have with Amber?" Coach asked. "Did she figure out one of your experiments and show you up?"

"No, nothing quite like that," Mr. Kistler said, snipping off the end of his words. "She's about to go on academic probation, Harry."

"What?" Amber thought she'd heard wrong.

"Wait a minute," Coach said, leaning forward. His chair banged the floor. "I know you're a tough teacher, Frank, but Amber Thomas is one hard-working student. How could her grades have fallen so fast?"

"It's a mystery to me. She's turned in the last three quizzes incomplete. It's not that she's giving the wrong answers. She's giving no answers. It's like she gives up in the middle and refuses to finish."

Amber burned inside. They were talking about her as if she weren't even there. "They were just quizzes," she said, realizing at once how stupid it sounded.

"I told my class from Day One that quizzes count," explained Mr. Kistler. He swung back to face Coach. "The bottom line right now is that if Amber doesn't make at least a ninety-eight on her midterm Monday, she'll be off the team until she brings up her grades."

"Ninety-eight?" Amber hoped she'd heard him wrong.

"Frank," Coach pleaded, "you know we have an important meet next week." It was the coach's turn to be irritated. "Is there any way to deal with this after our meet is over?"

"Not the way I see it. I'm sorry to spring this on you. I kept thinking she'd get back on track." He turned a crooked grin on Amber. "Everybody knows you have what it takes, Amber." He glanced at his watch. "I've got to run."

"I'll come with you," Coach said. As he left, Coach whispered, "As for you, I'll see you later."

She waited until Coach and Mr. Kistler left, deep in conversation, probably about her. *And so what?* She deserved to be talked about. Amber Thomas had never made anything lower than a B+ in her whole life. She started to go, when she heard a clang, the sound of metal on metal. "Who's there?" she asked, her heart pounding. She could almost feel the Stranger watching her. "Come out!" she screamed.

Two heads popped up from behind a pile of pool equipment. Morgan stood up. Then Alex got up and sprinted out of the junk room. Alex walked over to Morgan, who bit her lip and lifted her hand in a half-wave. "It's not what you think, Amber," Morgan said quickly. "We weren't trying to eavesdrop or spy or anything. Alex and I were talking, and we lost track of time. Then it was too late to go to our next class. Then we heard Kistler's whine. So we hid. I'm sorry."

How much did you hear, Morgan? And how much did Alex hear? The last thought was ten times worse than the first. If Alex had heard that Amber was in trouble, she'd probably spread it all over the school. "I knew Alex would get you in trouble if you kept hanging out with her, Morgan. I'll bet you've never cut class before."

"It's not Alex's fault!" Morgan's eyes teared up. "She's got so much going on, Amber, and she's just starting to open up. Did you know she moved here because her parents fought all the time? That's why she lives with her grandparents."

Amber didn't have room to feel sorry for anyone but herself. "So you take her side instead of mine?"

Morgan sighed. "Alex says I'm taking *your* side. She called me 'an Amber clone,' or 'president of the Amber Fan Club.' There shouldn't be *sides* anyway. We're all on the same team."

"Right," Amber said. "Except maybe not for long." Morgan was still talking when Amber walked off. She had the urge to just keep walking—down the hall, past chemistry, past the office, and out the door. She wouldn't do it—not good old' reliable Amber Thomas. That's how her teammates had always thought of her—until now.

chapter.6

Amber felt so depressed, she didn't even want to fight her way through the Edgewood High cafeteria. The lunchroom was decorated in gray—gray walls, gray floor, and gray counters. Long tables formed four straight lines until students shoved them into circles, making room for their cliques. To get hot lunch or pizza, she'd have to shove into one of the lines and hold her own against line-jumpers.

Instead, Amber plopped at the nearest empty table, not even saving seats for her friends. But as if tables had invisible place cards, most kids knew who sat where, and nobody sat down at their table. Closing her eyes, Amber listened to chairs squeak against the floor, the clatter of fallen forks, the clanging of spoons.

Amber watched Bren work the room, moving from table to

table, joking with someone at each table until she finally plopped across from Amber. Jamie followed quietly behind her.

"I see the mystery meat is well done today," Bren said, eyeing Jamie's plate as they slid in beside Amber.

"It's not as bad as you might think," Jamie offered. "You might want to try meat and vegetables sometime. I get enough junk food at the Gnosh Pit when I'm working. When do you get enough junk food, Bren? Give me nachos and ladyfingers any day compared to that . . . that . . . casserole-type-mom's-cooking kind of food. In fact—"

"Break it up you two!" Maya scooted in across from them. "We've got better things to talk about than cafeteria food." Maya stared at the empty spot where Amber's tray should have been. "Amber, where's your food?"

Amber was relieved. If Morgan had overheard the discussion in Coach's office, she apparently hadn't told Maya about it.

"Good question," Amber said, getting to her feet. "The lines are shorter now." She turned and rammed into somebody.

"Amber!" Morgan cried, giving her a weak, strained smile.

If Amber hadn't been sure before, she was now. Morgan knew everything. And in minutes, the other girls would drag it out of her whether Amber stuck around or not. Amber bolted for the pizza line.

As Amber walked off, she heard Maya: "Morgan, you look like you just lost your puppy, then lied about it. Spill, little sister!"

Amber didn't really care if Morgan told them she was flunking chemistry. They'd find out soon enough anyway. She got her plain cheese pizza and walked slowly back to the table, where the girls were leaned forward in a huddle. Amber set down her tray and slid in, feeling all eyes on her.

"So?" Maya began. "Tell me my little sister is wrong. Tell me Amber Thomas is not flunking Kistler's class."

Amber had to swallow tears. She stared at her pizza until she thought she might be sick. She didn't trust herself to answer without breaking down and bawling like a baby.

"This has something to do with that Jake Smith and the quiz you took a dive on this morning, doesn't it?" Bren asked. "I saw you during class. I was going to give you a hard time, but then I saw you turn your paper over early, and I couldn't figure out what was happening."

"Took a dive? You flunked again on *purpose?*" Maya was getting louder with each word. "You are putting the invitational meet at risk, and it's because of Jake Smith? Are you out of your mind?"

"I told you. It's complicated," Amber began. "By the time I realized what Jake was doing, he had cheated off of me lots of times. I felt like I'd become his accomplice. At least I thought Kistler would see it that way. I told Jake to stop, but he didn't. I tried to hide my paper from him, but you know how those tables are set up. It's impossible to completely hide if someone really wants to see your paper."

"OK, OK, but exactly when did you start falling the quizzes?" asked Maya.

"I didn't really mean to fail. I just got frustrated and started turning over my paper so Jake couldn't get any more answers from me. I figured he'd get bored and go cheat off of someone else or fill in his own answers or something. It seemed like I would be able to finish the last few answers just before Kistler called for the papers."

"Amber, why didn't you tell one of us so we could help you figure out what to do?" asked Jamie.

"I thought I could handle it. Besides, I didn't want to cause trouble with Jake. His family's had trouble enough, and our parents are good friends. I just kept thinking it would get better. I really thought I could handle it."

Maya had been stewing all the way through Amber's explanation. Now she slammed down her drink. "Nice job handling it yourself! And I'll tell you this, Amber Thomas. This is about more than you and your parents. This is about the whole swim team, including Coach. You better find a way to ace that test on Monday. And if it means ignoring Jake Smith in chemistry, then you ignore him! It's his problem anyway. You're not intentionally letting him cheat. Whatever you have to do, you better make the grade. You have to swim us to a win Tuesday night!"

Amber was blown away. "Maya, you don't want me to *let* him cheat, do you? I mean, how can I let somebody use me to do something wrong?"

"What's more wrong, Amber? I think it's wrong to let down your teammates who have worked hard to win. Think about that when you're thinking about what's right and wrong." Maya's voice started to shake.

"Wait a minute, Maya," said Bren. "There's more going on here than Amber's telling you. Tell them, Amber. Tell them about the e-mail you got last night."

For just a second, tears came into Amber's eyes. *How could a day go so wrong?* "I do think that maybe it was Jake that sent that e-mail."

"What e-mail are you talking about?" Jamie asked.

That was the last thing Amber felt like talking about.

Bren answered for her. "Last night Amber got a sort of sinister e-mail from someone called the Stranger. It said, 'You'll get yours.' She thinks it was Jake."

"I thought it might have been Jake threatening me so that I'd give him all the answers today. Now I'm almost sure it's Jake because today during our experiment he said almost that very phrase. I just —"

"Well, look who we have here," Jamie called out quickly as Jake Smith himself walked up to the table.

Jake leaned both hands on the table across from Amber. "Well, here's my lab partner spending some time with her girls. I just wanted to remind you to study hard this weekend for that midterm on Monday. I hear it's a tough one."

Amber played it cool. "Jake, you go be a big boy and study for yourself. It's something new called 'taking responsibility.'"

Maya stormed around the table to confront Jake. She

whipped the hard copy of the e-mail out of her pocket and flapped it in his face. "Let me tell you something, Jake Smith. If you are that small that you have to threaten somebody over the Internet, then you are the most shady, cowardly guy I've ever met!"

Jake grabbed the paper out of Maya's hand. "I'm not threatening anybody," he said. Then he read the message: "'You'll get yours.' What does that mean? I didn't write this. What address did it come from?"

"There's not an address. That's why we thought . . . we think you sent it," Maya answered.

Jake studied the e-mail printout. "I can tell you this right now: I'm sure not going to be hitting a stupid site called TodaysGirls.com. Get real." He crumpled the paper and spiked it into Jamie's plate before he walked away.

Maya looked at Amber. "You better deal with this, and you better be out of the threat of probation by the end of the class Monday morning. That's all I'm saying. Don't expect me at your house tonight or any other time until you get this all fixed." Maya huffed out of the lunchroom.

chapter.7

Amber flipped on her computer, closing her eyes and listening to the rhythm of its beeps and tones. They were as familiar as a friend's voice on the phone. When she opened her eyes, she smiled at her screen with its TodaysGirls.com wallpaper. She deliberately left the computer idle until the screen started falling apart like a jigsaw puzzle. This was her favorite screen saver, but today it looked just the way she felt—like everything was falling apart.

She logged on to the Web site and scrolled through her e-mail until her eyes stopped on an item from the Stranger. *Oh great. Now what?* she thought.

The first thing she noticed when she opened the mail was the 4:15 A.M. send time. *Can't you do something better at that hour than threaten me? Wouldn't you rather be sleeping?*

She opened the message:

Your time is coming.

Amber wanted to scream. As a reflex, she hit *reply* and started typing fast.

Leave me alone! I don't know who you are but GET AWAY FROM ME. Don't write me ever again.

She hit the *enter* key furiously then watched as the screen informed her that the Stranger's address had permanent fatal errors in it and her message couldn't be delivered.

Talk about fatal errors. It wasn't just the e-mail address that had fatal errors. The whole situation was blowing up in her face. Now the swim meet was on the line. Besides that, Maya was mad at her.

"Hi hon!" Amber's mom called from the doorway. "Whatcha' working on?"

Amber quickly escaped out of the e-mail and the mailbox list and mustered a smile before she looked up at her mom. "I'm about to start on next week's Thought for the Day for the Web site."

Amber's mom walked across the room to where Amber sat at her computer desk. Anyone who saw them together knew immediately that they were related in some way. If her mother wore her hair longer, she would have looked just like Amber. They both had striking green eyes that almost everyone mentioned when they first met either of them. Amber knew she'd picked up a lot more than eye color from her mom. Her mother cared about everyone around her and wanted to please these people who were important to them. Mom found it hard to say no to people, just as Amber was having a hard time saying no to Jake.

Mom sat down on the side of Amber's bed, crossed her legs, and smiled at her daughter. "Tell me about the Thought for the Day, Amber. I think it's great that you're doing this."

Amber looked at her mom and imagined for a second how great it would feel to tell her about the Stranger, and Jake, and Mr. Kistler, and the swim meet. She knew her mom would want to know. Her mom could probably even help. Amber wanted to start talking instead of holding it all in. But why should her mother worry?

Amber simply answered the question. "It's easy, really. I usually write five short thoughts for the week. Mostly they're just Bible verses and a few questions that apply them to everyday stuff that happens. The first time the girls log on, Monday through Friday at least, that day's thought pops up. They can just cancel the window or escape out if they want to, but I think they read it."

"That's impressive. Do you ever have a hard time thinking of what to write, or does it come easily?"

"It's not usually hard, though today might be a challenge. I have a big midterm Monday and a busy week, so I thought I'd get all of next week done before the girls come over tonight and the studying starts tomorrow."

"How many girls are coming, everyone on your Web site?" Mom asked.

"I don't think Maya's coming, but Bren and Jamie are."

"Is Maya busy?"

"Maya's always busy. I'm sure we'll talk this weekend, though." Amber avoided a messy spot again.

"Well, don't you work too hard, babe. Now that's something I never have to say to your brother, do I?"

They both laughed. "No, Mom. He's got 'taking it easy' down to a science. I'm having fun, though, even if the site is a lot of work."

As her mother headed for the door, Amber felt her opportunity for getting some support fading away. "Mom, I was wondering what you thought about something."

Mrs. Thomas turned around. "Sure. You can ask me anything. You know that."

Amber stood on the edge of a high dive, trying to get up the courage to plunge into the important questions she needed answers to. In that split second, though, she backed up and climbed back down the ladder to lower ground. "Do you have any suggestions for next week's Bible verses?"

"Hmmm, off the top of my head? If you haven't already used

it, you could start with Proverbs 3:5–6. That's always been one of my favorites. In fact, you could probably do a whole week on just those verses." Mrs. Thomas smiled at her daughter. "Anything else, babe?"

"No, but that helps. Thanks."

"I'll send the girls up when they get here." Mrs. Thomas shut the door behind her.

Amber turned back to the monitor, where her TodaysGirls wallpaper had already fallen apart and been re-created several times. There were only a few disconnected puzzle pieces on the screen. She quickly moved the mouse to keep those last pieces from falling apart. Maybe if she had talked to her mom, the process of her own life falling apart could have been stopped. *I'll just have to handle it myself,* she thought. But she had to wonder if that was really the best way.

She felt tears of frustration sting her eyes as she opened the Stranger's e-mail again. For just a minute she considered the possibility that the Stranger might not have a connection with Edgewood High. He could be a really scary someone. The truth was, Amber didn't know which would scare her more, to think she had been hacked in by some adult who needed to get a life, or by Jake Smith, who was currently ruining her life. Whichever it was, she didn't feel completely safe in her own room anymore, whether her computer was plugged into the wall or not.

Enough of this! I have things to do. Amber opened the edit screen for the Thoughts for the Day. She alt-tabbed to her Bible

Concordance program and entered "Proverbs 3:5–6." Immediately the screen showed her the verses.

> Trust the Lord with all your heart.
> Don't depend on your own understanding.
> Remember the Lord in everything you do.
> And he will give you success.
>
> PROVERBS 3:5–6

Success . . . , Amber thought. *That's what I need. I feel so lost, and I can't tell if I'm doing the right thing or not.*

She pasted the first line into the Thoughts for the Day screen for Monday.

Trust the Lord with all your heart.
Don't depend on your own understanding. Proverbs 3:5
    Ever feel like you've lost your way? Try trusting God instead of yourself.

Amber had been sitting on the front edge of her seat. She leaned back and rested her head against the back of her chair and stared at the words. *Trust the Lord. How do I trust God?* She closed her eyes and prayed, "God, I haven't been trusting you. I guess I have been depending on my own understanding. I've been trying to figure all of this out. Isn't that what I'm supposed to do? Isn't that taking responsibility for my life?"

When she opened her eyes to work again, she wasn't sure which was her greatest concern—finishing her feature on the Web page or finding answers for her own life. She pasted in the next line of the verses:

Remember the Lord in everything you do.

How do I remember the Lord? Amber asked herself. *I guess praying is remembering. When I pray, I'm letting him in, and I'm admitting that I need his help.*

Amber felt something familiar inside. It was like what she felt when she heard her pastor say something that really clicked with her. Her heart started beating a little faster, and her spirit said an excited, "Yes!"

Hadn't she been taught since she was a baby that God wanted to help with her problems? Why hadn't she thought about this before? Until now, she hadn't prayed about Jake or about chemistry or about the Stranger or anything. Amber realized she was smiling again, and it felt good. Nothing was really different. The Stranger and Jake were still around, but she didn't feel so alone.

She decided to start over and do just as her mom had said, stretching the two verses out over the whole week. She'd list a line of the verses for each day, then the whole thing on Friday.

Trust the Lord with all your heart.
Are your plans falling apart? Are your best-laid plans

making things worse rather than better? Trust God to bring it all together in the end.

Don't depend on your own understanding.

Why do we think we know so much when we have so much to learn? We try to figure life out, but God is the only one who understands it all. Trust him when life is not fair and things are not going your way. Tough teacher? Bad friend? Family problems? He'll know what to do.

Remember the Lord in everything you do.

Remembering God means believing that he is, and that he will do what he says. Take time to pray about everything you do. Take time to look him in the face. If you do, then you'll find him looking right back at you.

And he will give you success.

How much farther will we get in life if we let God lead the way? When you can't tell which way to turn, let God fulfill his promises to you. Which problems can you not solve? All you have to do is ask the Lord.

For Friday, she listed the whole verse and wrote:

Maybe one of the keys to getting through high school alive is in these verses: trusting God and letting him lead us. After all, life's hard enough without doing it by ourselves. Trust God to help you through.

Amber particularly liked those last two sentences. She sat looking out the window for a while, rolling the words around in her mind. *Life's hard enough without doing it by ourselves. Trust God to help you through.*

chapter.8

Hey, girl! Turn off that computer, and let's have some fun. It's Friday night!" Bren said as she and Jamie bounced into Amber's room. "We're ready to do something. What are you up for?"

Amber sat up straight and started typing commands on her keyboard. "Let me close out here, and then we can decide." She paused and then admitted, "I heard from the Stranger again."

Jamie's face changed from carefree to concerned in one instant. "You must be so worried, Amber, with everything that's going on. I'm so sorry. What did he say?"

Amber continued shutting down programs as she talked. "This time he said, 'Your time is coming.' What do you think he meant by that?"

Bren joined in, "Well, if it's Jake, then he's probably talking about the test on Monday."

"Oh yeah," said Amber quietly. "What if it's not Jake?"

"You need to tell somebody about this, Amber," Jamie insisted.

"I think things are going to work out. I don't know how, but somehow." The screen went dark, and Amber swiveled around and flashed a smile at her friends. "Now, what do you have in mind for our evening of rest and relaxation?" she asked, sliding from her chair and stretching out on the floor.

"Well, I was just thinking," Bren began, her eyes glittering. "It's been quite a while since we messed with Coach's mind. I think tonight's the night."

"I'm up for it," Amber volunteered. "What do you have in your bag of tricks?"

Bren straddled the computer chair, then swiveled around to face the girls. "You know how Coach *loves* his yard and keeps it so spotless? Well, there are still loads of leaves in Amber's side yard . . ."

"Thanks to Ryan," Amber added.

"Let's bag up those leaves," Bren said, smiling, "and then take them over to Coach's perfect yard and scatter them out. Wouldn't he just have a fit?"

"Won't he catch us?" Jamie protested.

Bren rolled her eyes. "No, he won't. He's out of town scouting Baldwin. They're swimming against us next week, and they have a makeup meet tonight."

"Won't it take a long time?" Amber asked.

"A couple of hours, maybe. Let's do it."

Suddenly a fourth voice boomed in: "If that's not the *stupidest* plan I've ever heard. You girls just have too much time on your hands." It was Ryan, sweaty and dirty, standing in the doorway, leaning one hand on the doorframe. He looked at them as if he were seeing someone walking barefoot in the snow.

Amber knew exactly what to do in this situation. "Bren and Jamie, you have just got to remember to close the door behind you. You never know what stray might wander in." As she spoke, she walked to the door and swiftly slammed it in Ryan's face.

"Hey!" Ryan's voice sounded loud and clear through the door. "You almost gave me a black eye!"

"Ryan! Leave the girls alone!" Amber's mom called from the kitchen.

Ryan's bedroom door slammed shut, and Amber knew she had won the round. The girls headed down to the garage for supplies. Mrs. Thomas said she was thrilled that the girls were going to clean up the side yard. The girls didn't go into great detail about their motivation. They didn't lie about it. They just didn't offer any extra information.

In the garage, they gathered the flashlights off the three hooks by the door. They collected rakes, leaf bags, and gloves from the back wall clamps. Before the last bit of light was gone from the sky, they had filled six 30-gallon bags of leaves from the side yard of the house. Each girl stuck a flashlight in her back pocket and carried a bag of leaves in each hand. Like three spies carrying contraband, they began the three-quarter-mile walk to Coach Short's manicured front yard.

"I'm glad leaves don't weigh much," Jamie said as they rounded the last corner.

Bren stooped over and peered around the bushes. "Let me go first and make sure he's gone." Within a minute, she walked back around the bushes. "We're safe. Let's go."

Scattering the leaves took a lot less time than gathering them. The girls had the yard covered within fifteen minutes. As the last daylight faded, they turned on their flashlights to survey their work and make some adjustments. At one point Jamie was shining all three flashlights so that Amber and Bren could get leaves in the most out-of-reach places. They decided Coach deserved a challenge. For a final flourish, they took all his hanging pansies and hung them across the street on his neighbor's mailbox.

"Looks really bad," said Jamie. "I'm not sure he'll be able to handle his precious yard so out of whack."

"He's going to freak!" Bren added, giggling.

Suddenly, Amber heard a car. "He's coming! I think I hear his car down the road!" Amber took off at full speed, dashing behind bushes, through the backyards toward her house. Jamie and Bren were right behind her, gasping for air as they laughed and panted themselves into spasms.

Amber had grown up in this neighborhood, so she knew most of the available cut-throughs and bike paths. Bren and Jamie kept pace with her almost every step of the way. They jumped over trash cans and slid sideways between fence posts. They ignored barking dogs and dodged hissing cats. They didn't slow down until they were back on Amber's block.

"Amber, what are you doing?" Bren asked between breaths. "There's no way he could have been back so soon. Why did you put us through that?"

"It sure sounded like his car," Amber said in mock innocence. "And didn't we have a good run? I haven't run that hard or laughed that hard in a long time."

"I'm glad you enjoyed it," said Jamie holding her side and wincing as she breathed. "Let's get back to your house. How much farther is it?"

As they entered the garage, Bren and Jamie, put their flashlights by the door. Amber put away the rakes and threw the used bags in the recycle bin.

Inside, Mrs. Thomas offered them hot chocolate for their hard work. The girls giggled their way into the den with a bag of marshmallows while Amber's mom heated the cocoa.

The furniture in Amber's den was furniture a person could fall *into*. Jamie and Amber lay back on opposite ends of the couch across from the fireplace where the gas logs were burning.

Bren pounced on the overstuffed chair. She opened the bag and grabbed two oversize marshmallows and drew a face on each of them with a ballpoint pen. One face had a big frown and a bald head. The other had a big smile and some straggly hair. She held each marshmallow in thumb and forefinger like puppets. Then she squeezed them slightly as she acted out a marshmallow play.

"I want to know who messed up my yard!" said Bren in a low, gruff voice, squeezing the bald marshmallow. "Jamie do you know anything about this?"

In a squeaky voice, Bren spoke for her other puppet. "Oh, no sir, Harry. I don't know *who* would pull such an inconsiderate prank. I'll be your spy and find the villains."

"I resent that!" non-marshmallow Jamie called out, laughing.

"Well, you better, you young whippersnapper," Bren continued in her Harry-voice. "I had that yard perfectly spotless, and I won't stand for it! Do you hear me? I won't stand for it! And where are my pansies?"

"Pansies?" said the squeaky puppet in Bren's right hand. "Are you sure you had pansies, Harry, because I thought you only had leaves in your yard, and—"

"Here you go, girls," said Mrs. Thomas, carrying in three steaming snowman mugs of real cocoa. "You've already brought the marshmallows in, right?"

Amber looked over at Bren, expecting to see her with her arms lifted and her two puppets dangling in midair. Not Bren, though. She was smiling innocently, hands and puppets out of sight. Bren's quick change made Amber laugh harder than the puppet show had.

"I left some spoons in case you need to stir your hot chocolate to cool it off," Amber's mom said as she walked back toward the kitchen. "Oh, and Bren?"

"Yes, Mrs. Thomas?"

"Your coach does have pansies, doesn't he?"

Bren's eyes were brimming over with tears as she held her laughter in check. When she spoke, her voice was the picture of calm. "Coach Short *always* has pansies, Mrs. Thomas. I'm sure this year is no exception."

"You girls have fun," Amber's mom said as she closed the door behind her.

The girls fell into crumpled piles of laughter. Bren threw the squished puppets at her friends, which started an all-out marshmallow war. By the time the room was reclaimed for peace, the hot chocolate was warm chocolate and Amber's side hurt from laughing.

The girls talked for a while by the fire. They talked about swimming, and grades, and boys, and teachers. Finally, Jamie brought the conversation back around to the e-mail. "Amber, I know you like to handle stuff on your own, but I'm worried about this. Is there any way I can talk you into telling Harry or Mr. Kistler or your mom about it to see if they can help?"

Jamie's concerns made a lot of sense to Amber. She didn't watch the news all the time, but she heard enough to know that the world isn't always a safe place. Still, she was hoping for a happy ending. "Let's just give it until Monday. Let me get the test out of the way, so I'm in good standing with my grades. Then I'll talk to Mom about Jake. Since I'm ninety-nine percent sure that he's the source of the e-mails, I bet they stop after the test."

"I hope you're right, Amber," said Bren. "Just in case,

though, don't do anything stupid, all right?"

Amber glared at Bren. "Bren Mickler! When have you ever known me to do anything stupid?"

Amber expected Bren to laugh, but instead she answered quietly, "Never . . . until this Jake thing, Amber."

The girls sat silently in front of the fire for a while before Amber said, "This will all be over Monday. I really believe that. Let's don't worry about it until then."

They heard a car pull into the driveway. "That's Mom," said Bren. "She said she'd stop by when she got finished shopping. I guess there's nothing left in the stores. What do you think, Jamie?"

"It's the only reason I can think of that she'd stop," said Jamie right on cue. She and Bren smiled at Amber.

"That'll be us one day, girls," said Amber, smiling back.

Jamie faked surprise as she finally stood up from the comfortable sofa. "One day? I think Bren can keep up with Mrs. Mickler *any* day, don't you?"

"Hey now!" protested Bren while she gathered their mugs and leftover marshmallows.

Bren and Jamie called out their thanks to Mrs. Thomas as they passed through the kitchen on their way to the car.

Amber hugged both of her friends as they said good-bye. She smiled just thinking about what Coach's face must have looked like when he got home that night.

chapter.9

The Sunday morning sun shone warm for late October, but did little to ease the crisp chill in the air.

"Hey, girl!" Amber called out the car window to Jamie. "I'll meet you inside after I park the car."

Amber let her mom out of the car at the front doors to their church. Then she circled around to park by the youth building, where she knew Jamie would be waiting.

"Hi there, Amber!" said Jamie. "Sweet outfit. Has Mrs. Mickler been shopping for you?"

Amber looked down at her pale green sweater dress as if she couldn't remember what she was wearing. "Jamie, you've seen this before. But thanks for thinking I look like I have anything to do with the *fabulous* Micklers."

"Where were you yesterday?" Jamie asked as they started

walking toward the youth room. "I signed on several different times to chat, and you were never there."

"Believe it or not, I stayed off the computer yesterday." Amber lowered her voice almost to a whisper. "I even unplugged it. I didn't want the Stranger getting anywhere near me while I studied for the midterm."

"Amber!" said Jamie, laughing at the same time. "You know he can't get to you through the computer. I can't believe somebody as logical as you would be so silly."

Amber stopped just outside of their Sunday school room. "You haven't heard anything yet. I'm not only becoming silly; I'm becoming paranoid. Yesterday, I was positive I saw the same car sitting out in front of my house for way too long. I kept looking out the window like one of those people in a witness protection program. Finally, I realized it was the work car my dad was using while his was in the shop. Go figure."

"Amber, you're scared of the Stranger, aren't you? Why else would you be feeling like this?"

Amber looked at Jamie before she answered honestly, "I'm a little wigged out. But in my head I know things are going to be OK."

Amber walked past Jamie into their classroom and started talking to some other friends. Sunday school started with Bible verses on the board and discussion groups around the room, and it ended with a game. The teacher divided the room into two teams: the Shirts and the Coats. The verse for the day had been

Luke 6:29: "If anyone slaps you on your cheek, let him slap the other cheek too. If someone takes your coat, do not stop him from taking your shirt."

The game was set up like a TV game show where each team could discuss the right answers among themselves. There was one fake buzzer per team and a stopwatch manned by an adult. The leader described situations where someone asked the kids for something. The Coats had to make up a response that would reflect a selfish attitude, giving only what the person asked for and no more. The Shirts had to make up a response that would reflect a Christlike attitude, giving away their shirts *and* their coats.

Amber was on the Shirt team. She soon realized that she was good at figuring out how to give people more than they asked for. The activity caused her to rethink her situation at school. She wondered if she was looking at this whole "Jake thing" the wrong way. Maybe she really would be helping him if she let him copy answers from time to time. It's not like she would *help* him cheat, but what if she just didn't notice?

On her way to the sanctuary, she mentioned it to Jamie. "What?" Jamie said with a scowl. "Amber, I don't think you can take that verse to mean that if someone asks you for an answer on a quiz that you should give him your whole test as well. Get real!"

Amber tried to interrupt her friend. "I'm just saying—"

"Stop," said Jamie, and Amber did. "I've got to go. The

Gnosh Pit is opening early today. Why don't you come down later and we can talk about this some more. For now, think it through. Your life is crazy enough without deciding you should help the people who are taking advantage of you."

Jamie rushed out to the parking lot, leaving her friend in midsentence. Amber sat through church, half listening and half thinking through her options. The preacher kept referring to a Bible verse where Jesus said, "I was a stranger and you took me in." Every time Amber heard the word *stranger,* her stomach flipped. Then her thoughts would start rolling around in her head again, distracting her from anything else she was hearing.

When Amber got back home after church, her study notes and books were still stacked across the bottom of her bed. Her computer was still unplugged. The no-longer-suspicious car was still parked in front of her house. Not much had changed from the day before. She felt a little more confused, though.

At lunch, Amber told her parents about the Shirts and Coats game in Sunday school. Ryan rolled his eyes the whole time she was talking, which made her drag out the conversation even longer than she normally would. Anything that annoyed Ryan was worth savoring. When she finally finished, she asked, "What do you guys think about it? How much is giving away too much, and how much is giving away too little?"

Her father, as always, gave the business answer. "There's an expression we use in the world of commerce: 'giving away your shirt.' I guess it might come from that Bible verse. Normally, though, when someone talks about giving away his shirt in business, it's not a good thing. It usually means you gave away too much and didn't take care of yourself. I don't think Jesus would have taught people to do that."

Amber's mom, as usual, headed for the touchy-feely answer. "I think that's the same verse that talks about if someone slaps your cheek, turn the other one, isn't it?"

"Now I like that!" Ryan added. "Let's talk about that verse the next time I have you backed against the wall for a pounding."

Amber smirked at her brother as she said, "Go on, Mom. What do you think that means?"

Her mother looked over Amber's head and half-closed her eyes. This is what she always did when she was thinking. Amber caught herself doing the same thing sometimes. "I think it's about your attitude. I think it's about whether you really, sincerely, want to help people, or whether you just try to get them off your back."

Neither answer helped Amber decide whether she should be more helpful toward Jake, but they went a long way toward driving Ryan crazy. That made Amber's day just a little sweeter.

As Amber was cleaning off the table, her dad said, "Listen, pumpkin. I'm going to take Mom out tonight for a while. You and Ryan will be fine here, won't you?"

Amber's first thought was, *Pumpkin? Where do parents get these names for their kids who are not round and orange?* Her next thought was *Alone with Ryan?* "Actually, Dad, I was thinking about going to the Gnosh Pit for a while to hang out while Jamie works. Would that be OK? I'm sure Ryan would rather do something besides stay home with me."

"Well, how nice of you, Amber, to think of your brother's enjoyment," said her father. "Is this your form of giving him your shirt, or is this a coat thing?"

Amber smiled as she carried the last stack of dishes into the kitchen for her mom to load into the dishwasher. As long as she got to get out of the house, she didn't care what anybody thought.

chapter.10

When Amber walked into the Gnosh, everything about it was buzzing. Jamie and two other servers were working all the tables, plus the counter. There was a birthday party in the back corner, including noisemakers, pointed hats, and a birthday cake with sparklers for candles. Amber stood just inside the door while she adjusted to the activity level.

"Hi, Amber!" Jamie called out as she rushed past with a tray full of burgers, fries, and ketchup bottles. "Follow me!"

Amber followed, sure that any minute she would be catching the tray's contents with the front of her shirt. She couldn't see anything but Jamie's back as they swiveled and swerved between tables toward the opposite side of the restaurant from the birthday party. Finally Jamie stopped short, and Amber barely kept from barreling over her. As Jamie put down the tray,

Amber looked around her to see a table with three young faces and one old and familiar one.

"Coach Short?" Amber asked. "You come to the Gnosh Pit?" She studied his expression for signs of anger or revenge. But he didn't seem the least bit angry about the leaves they'd dumped. Maybe he hadn't figured out who did it yet.

"This is absolutely my favorite diner, Amber," answered the coach, winking at Jamie. "The food's OK, but the service—now that is *par excellence.*"

"Gimme-a-break," said Jamie all in one syllable. "Mrs. Coach is out of town, and he got stuck with getting dinner for the boys." She grinned at each of Coach's sons. "So he brought them here for me to feed. Don't believe him if he says anything different, Amber."

Coach lowered his head, but glanced up at the girls. "I'm caught. I admit it." Then he asked, "Amber, will you join us? We're like sitting in the center ring of a circus, but the trapeze act is pretty good."

Jamie had already scooted the boys around the circular booth to make room for Amber beside Coach Short. Then she turned around to bus some tables nearby. The thought crossed Amber's mind that Jamie might have planned this whole scenario in hopes that Amber would confide in Coach. Amber smiled over at the coach as she sat down. Maybe she would ask his opinion about Jake. Maybe Jamie had a good plan.

Before Amber could ask anything, though, Jamie swung

back from the other tables with her pen and pad in hand, smacking some fake gum like she was an old-time diner waitress. "So what'll it be for you, ma'am?"

Coach's boys giggled at Jamie, who was like the big sister they'd always wanted.

"How about a burger and fries," said Amber, looking around at the plates already on the table. "That looks like the special of the day."

Jamie rolled her eyes as she walked away. "Burgers and fries. Burgers and fries. My whole life is burgers and fries."

"And ketchup!" called out Harrison Jr., Coach's eldest. "We need ketchup!" Jamie's head bobbed, which meant she had heard him. That was his cue to dive into his burger.

"How's it going, Amber?" asked Coach as he took the pickles and onions away from Nat's burger and the lettuce away from Chris's. "My younger boys are a little picky." Coach added the fixings to his sandwich. "I'm not picky," he added. "How's it going?" he asked one more time.

"You know about the big midterm Monday?" she began.

"Yes," was all he said. This was her cue to continue.

"So I studied all day yesterday. I don't think it will be a problem."

"Good," was the one-word answer this time. He wanted more.

"I'm psyched for the meet Tuesday night. What a great medley relay *that's* going to be, huh?"

"The best!" Coach agreed as he cut Chris's burger into

smaller pieces. His silence, though, let her know that he would wait until she *really* told him how things were going.

Jamie arrived with a plate of food. "Just as you like it, ma'am," she said through the same pretend gum as before. "Easy on the mayo, extra pickles, and lizard feet!" Jamie waved the plate in front of the boys' faces as she emphasized the last ingredient. All three laughed out loud whether their mouths were full of burgers or not.

"Thanks," said Amber. She knew that the lizard feet were really the sautéed mushrooms that Jamie had added without even asking. It was a wonderful thing to be friends with a server at a restaurant.

On the other side of the circle from Amber, Chris whispered into Nat's ear. Nat smiled, then whispered into Harry Jr.'s ear. He started laughing and whispered into his dad's ear. Coach listened for a second, then laughed loudly enough to win the attention of the tables on both sides. Amber knew something was about to be said at her expense. She wasn't sure exactly what, though.

"What did he say?" Amber asked, nodding toward Chris while she cut her burger in half.

"Believe it or not, he said he's never seen you with your clothes on," Coach Short answered, dropping his voice a few levels at the end so that he wouldn't be misunderstood by any dining neighbors.

"Chris!" said Amber, blushing, but understanding his mistake. "I think what you *meant* to say was that you've only seen me in my bathing suit, right?"

Chris's right hand was planted over his mouth to hold in his laughter and any other embarrassing thing he might say. He smiled and nodded at Amber. Coach, Nat, and Coach Jr. were still laughing as if this were the funniest joke they had heard in days.

Guys, Amber thought as she forked a few stray mushrooms. *They have the weirdest sense of humor.* While the boys still giggled, Amber placed a few mushrooms on each plate. Coach pushed his aside. Harry Jr. made a face. Nat and Chris stared at the mushrooms as if they were something far worse than lizard feet.

"So, Amber," Coach said as the laughter died in the face of the mushrooms, "how *is* it going?"

Before Amber could answer, Jamie plopped two plastic ketchup bottles down in the middle of the table. Then she did a double take at the mushroomed plates before she swooped away again. She wasn't at the table even long enough to create a distraction.

"There is something I've been wanting to get some opinions on," Amber confessed to Coach.

He looked over the boys' plates to be sure they were eating, then sat back and said, "Go ahead. Shoot. Opinions are free here."

"At church this morning we talked about how much we

should help people. We read that verse about if someone asks you for your coat, you should give them your shirt, too. What do you think about that?"

"Are you asking me if I agree with the Bible?" Coach clarified.

"No, not really," said Amber. "I know you aren't going to disagree with the Bible. But, how much should we help people? When is it OK to say no?"

Jamie dropped a few more fries on Nat's plate and took Chris up to sit at the counter so that Amber and Coach could talk without being interrupted.

"I'd probably give you a better answer, Amber, if you'd tell me a little about why you are asking."

Amber thought for a moment about how to focus her question without giving away too much information. "Well . . . what if someone you care about asks you for something you don't want to give?"

Coach's face showed immediate concern. He asked Harrison Jr. to take Nat to the rest room and wash off his hands and face, which were covered with ketchup. Once the boys were away from the table, he said, "Amber, is someone asking you to do something that is wrong?"

"I thought so at first," she answered. "In fact, I've gotten a little scared of this person."

"What is he asking you to do? You're scaring *me*."

"Coach, I didn't say it was a *he*."

"Sorry. Just testing."

"It's just a friend, really. At first, I was angry. Then I got sort of scared. Sometimes you think you know someone. Then all of a sudden you wonder if you know them at all."

"You're scaring me again, Amber. Can't you just tell me what's going on?"

"It's really not as big a deal as you think. After hearing that verse this morning I wondered if maybe my friend is asking for help and if maybe I've been selfish."

Coach finally realized that Amber was not going to budge from her no-tell position. He said, "The Bible does teach us to give to each other even when we have to sacrifice to do it. If your friend needs your help, then maybe you need to help him."

Nat and little Harrison dripped back to the table with a trail of water from both of Nat's shirtsleeves. Jamie followed their trail with a mop. Chris was riding piggyback as she mopped. She deposited him at the table and put one bill on the table for the food. "I figure Coach can pay for yours tonight. He owes me for baby-sitting anyway."

Coach nodded in agreement with Jamie's plan. He corralled the boys and headed them toward the door. Before he walked out, he looked Amber in the eyes and said, "You take care of yourself. Your friend may need help, but God doesn't ask us to do something we know is wrong to help someone. Remember this: *your time may be coming* when you need help *yourself.*"

With a wave, he was out the door. Amber was about to ask Jamie if she caught the connection between what Coach said and the Stranger's last e-mail, but once she looked at Jamie, she didn't have to ask a thing. Jamie had caught it loud and clear. Once they spotted the fear in each other's eyes, they burst out laughing.

Jamie shook her head. "You're making me paranoid now. For a second there I was stamping 'the Stranger' across Harry's head."

"Talk about strange. There wouldn't be anything stranger than that," Amber agreed.

chapter.11

Amber's footsteps echoed down the empty school hallway. She felt disoriented, as if she were underwater. It seemed like everything around her was moving slower and slower, but she was speeding up.

She passed the lab and the principal's office. She saw all the familiar places, but they seemed to be in the wrong places. Where were the lockers? Oh, there—but she couldn't remember her locker number . . . locker 98 . . . or . . . 72, or was it 78?

She gave up on the locker combination after sixty tries. *Sixty* tries? How long had she been standing there? And why weren't there any other kids? Then once she gave up, the locker opened by itself and the inside was a full-length mirror. In the mirror she could tell that she was . . . oh no . . . still in her nightgown!

Out of nowhere, Miss Roberts, the oldest English teacher in the whole wide world, appeared with zombie eyes. "Amber, where is your term paper, and where are your clothes?"

"Term paper? What term paper?" Amber began to panic. She didn't even have a class with Miss Roberts! At least, she didn't think she did. Was she supposed to have been in that class the whole semester and hadn't been going? Now *she* was slowing down and everything around her was speeding up. Miss Roberts was talking in a real fast voice like fast-forwarding a tape. Her voice got louder and shriller and *louder* and *shriller* until . . .

Amber realized she was hearing her alarm clock. She was in her own bedroom. It was a dream, or more like a nightmare. Thank goodness, it was over. She rolled over for just one more minute's sleep. When she opened her eyes the next time, the clock read, 5:00 A.M. The van would be there any minute! Talk about a nightmare!

There was not even time to irritate Ryan. Amber leaped from bed and grabbed her clothes. She pulled on blue sweats while she brushed her teeth. She washed her face and then threw on her sweatshirt. And thank goodness they had showers at school. Just as she found her bag, she heard the familiar honk in the driveway, then the doorbell, then Ryan yelling from under the covers, "Do they *have* to do that?"

As Amber walked down the sidewalk, leaves blew across her path. She remembered the prank she and Bren and Jamie had played on the coach. She tried not to smile, but remembering their secret, she didn't feel sleepy at all.

She threw her stuff in the back and, once again, crawled into the rear seat because Alex was in the front. When the closing door turned off the overhead light, she let her gaze meet Bren's. Without making a sound, she mouthed, "What did he say?" After all this time, Coach must have put two and two together.

Bren silently mouthed back, "Nothing."

She mouthed again, "What did he do?"

Bren shook her head from side to side.

Amber started to tell Bren that she had seen Coach the night before and he hadn't mentioned anything, when Coach broke in. "So what did you girls do over the weekend? Anything exciting?"

Amber and Bren were silent, but Alex and Morgan chattered away about Alex coming over Friday night and how boring the rest of the weekend was.

"Where is Maya this morning, again?" Amber asked Morgan.

"Dad got the VW running again, so she drove in. Jamie's with her. I can't believe Jamie gets up this early just to practice driving."

Suddenly the van turned too sharply and the girls leaned to the left and grabbed their books to keep them from tumbling everywhere. "Sorry 'bout that," Coach said. "With these crazy drivers on the road, I hate for any of you to be driving. Jamie isn't up just to practice driving, though. She and Bren are going to help me check times today. I've even asked them to suit up."

"And I, for one, am not happy about it," Bren said, looking out the window. "I've always thought you guys were freaks for putting on bathing suits in winter. Now I'm going to be one of you. It's unnatural, don't you think? I mean, unless you live in Sweden or somewhere where old people go soak in those hot springs places. I just don't get it."

"That's not Sweden is it?" asked Morgan.

Bren slowly turned her head toward Morgan. Very matter-of-factly she said, "No matter where it is, it's not here."

"Let's change the subject," said Amber.

"I've got a new subject." Coach Short offered. "How are you feeling about your midterm this morning, Amber?"

Amber froze. She hadn't given the midterm a thought yet this morning. It was the test that would determine the fate of the swim meet, and it was just hours away.

"Amber, you do remember that you have the test this morning, don't you?" Coach asked, and there was that worried tone riding his voice like a surfboarder.

"Yes, she does," Morgan answered for her, raising her voice with each word, "and we all know that Amber will ace the test, *don't we?*"

Amber was recovering from the shock that she could forget something important so easily. She nodded her head, slowly at first, then faster as she realized her friends needed some kind of confirmation that she had a handle on things. "Yes, we know that. I know the material, and I'm not worried. I'm going to do my best and trust that it will be enough. Thanks so *much* for your *heartfelt* concern that has *nothing* to do with winning the swim meet, right?"

"Yeah, yeah, yeah," said Coach. "You know I want you to do well, *and* I want to win that swim meet. Hey, Friday night I watched one of the teams you'll be swimming against. Pretty tough competition, if you ask me. And you *should be* asking me."

Amber's heart stopped when Coach mentioned Friday night. She wanted to look over at Bren, but she was so afraid they would act suspicious or something, that she just kept looking out the window as the van pulled in the parking lot. "I think we can handle them, Coach," was all she said.

In the locker room, everyone on the team was suited up except Alex. She was still running around with her clothes on.

"Why aren't you ready?" Morgan asked her.

"I thought I put my suit in my bag, but I can't find it. I don't think Gram would have taken it out. We hung it up in the junk room, but I've looked there three times and it's not—"

"Oh no!" Morgan said, her eyes open wide. "I bet I know what happened. Come on."

Morgan glared at Amber, who tried not to laugh. Jamie was smiling broadly. Morgan sighed and led Alex into the junk room. The team followed and stood at the door, peering in.

Morgan stood Alex directly in front of the refrigerator. Then she said, "Alex, remember what I was telling you about letting the upperclassmen have their privileges?"

Alex looked at Morgan like she was crazy. "Why bring that up now? And why are we in here? I told you I looked."

"You are about to get your first lesson in being the new kid."

"What do you mean?" asked Alex.

"Just look in the freezer."

Alex opened the freezer door. After the frost cleared, she reached in and brought out a crusted sheet of neon green. The shape looked more like a glacier than anything a human would wear. Alex rolled her eyes at them. "They froze my bathing suit? How am I supposed to be ready in time for practice?" Alex's suit was a sheet of ice.

"Don't be mad, Alex," Morgan begged. "It happens to every freshman."

The girls at the door applauded Alex's discovery, then burst into laughter.

"Show's over!" said Morgan, running over and shutting the door in their faces.

While Morgan and Alex were undoubtedly warming up Alex's suit, Amber gathered by the pool with the team. Coach called a huddle. "I've got some announcements," he said. "First of all, there might be a last-minute change in the lineup for the medley relay and for a few of the individual events. We'll know by this afternoon."

Several of the girls looked around at Amber with raised eyebrows. The news about her academic probation had spread like the juicy gossip that it was. "Just remember," continued Coach Short, "that the information you'll need will be posted on the main bulletin board."

Amber glanced at the team bulletin board. An odd light shone on the borders of the pegboard. Coach was using a flashlight for special effect. Amber figured this must have been his new toy. He twirled it, circled the board with his new light. With every announcement, Coach highlighted words and numbers. He used his toy to review regulations for grabstarts and the changes to the spectator area.

How come Coach is so hung up on a flashlight? Amber wondered. *Flashlight?* Amber swung around to see the flashlight in Coach's hand. For the second time that morning her heart almost stopped as she recognized the flashlight. Her last name, "Thomas," was clearly written on the side. Her dad had burned their name into every tool in the garage. The toy in Coach's hand was definitely from the Thomas garage, and there was only one way Coach could have gotten it. Someone must have dropped a flashlight Friday night!

Amber glanced over at Bren and Jamie. They didn't look like they had any idea of what was going on.

Coach droned on. "Our special effects today are thanks to Amber's dad, Mr. Thomas. He evidently left me this flashlight Friday night so I could use it this morning. Amber, will you thank your dad for me?"

Amber didn't answer. She watched Bren and Jamie to see when they were *ever* going to understand what was happening. Finally, it must have clicked. They looked like little kids who had been caught elbow-deep in the cookie jar.

"Amber?" Coach said sweetly. "You *will* tell your dad thanks, won't you?"

"Sure, Coach," Amber said, as if it were no big deal. She could be cool under pressure. She wasn't so sure, though, about her two dumbfounded friends.

"OK. That's it for announcements, everybody. Tell you what. We're going to try something new today. Usually our freshmen put out the lane markers, but we're going to give them a break. I've asked Bren and Jamie to suit up and join us. We'll let them take care of that while the rest of you do your stretches. Amber, I know you're good friends with the girls. Will you show them what to do and then help them in the pool?"

"Sure, Coach," Amber said, as if this were the most natural request he could have made of two non-team members and a junior on the team. She knew what he was up to, though. Coach had a nasty habit of dropping the temperature in the pool before a meet. He had dropped it over the weekend, from a comfy eighty-eight degrees to a bone-chilling seventy-eight. The three human leaf-blowers might as well be jumping into ice.

From experience, Amber knew that there was no easy way to enter a cold pool. The only decision was whether you wanted the pain all at once, or in slow death by inches. Amber dived in headfirst to get it over with. Coach might get revenge, but she wouldn't let him enjoy it any more than she had to.

Jamie and Bren, on the other hand, entered the pool inch by inch. They shivered more with every step, waving their hands in the air like prissy was in style. "Come on, you guys!" Amber called from the middle of the lane. "Don't make it too sweet for him." She spied the coach watching from the sidelines. He wore a huge smile. It was hard to imagine how he could've enjoyed himself more.

Finally, the lane markers were stretched the length of the pool. Bren had swum the length of the pool without even getting her hair wet. Her lips were blue, though, and she couldn't speak because she was shivering so hard. Jamie looked a little better than Bren.

One thing they knew: Coach would never say another word to them about the leaves. In his mind, he had won. Besides, he had always told them, "Revenge is best when it's served up cold." This time he had served it up practically frosted over.

chapter.12

After practice, Amber headed to class to ace her chemistry midterm. She glanced at her hard copy of the verse from her Thought for the Day: "Trust the Lord with all your heart." *Help me trust you, God. Please keep Jake from being the cheater that he is. Please keep me safe from the Stranger if he's not Jake. Help me find the success you have promised me.*

When Amber walked into the room, she breathed a quiet "Thank you." Mr. Kistler had removed all the equipment from the lab tables. That meant that he had a clear view of every student, including Jake Smith, cheater *extraordinaire*. If she couldn't make Jake take responsibility for his own work, maybe Mr. Kistler's dark, beady eyes would be an incentive.

"Hi there, Amber," Jake said with a smile, taking his seat on the lab stool. "Study hard?"

"Yes I did, Jake. How about you?"

"I studied." Jake looked tired and a little sad. "My dad had a bad weekend. I didn't get as much done as I wanted to. I guess I'm saying that I'm in trouble on this one."

Amber's heart went out to Jake. She wanted to help him. At the same time, she wanted him to help himself. "Have you noticed how Kistler cleaned up in here? He can see everything that happens. You're on your own, Jake, no matter how you or I feel about it." Then, to soften the blow, she said, "I bet you'll do better than you think."

"You can be really cold, Amber," Jake said quietly. "You're the stranger, if you ask me."

The class groaned in waves as the test papers filtered to the back of the room. Frank Kistler's chemistry midterm was one of the most famous exams at Edgewood. The wording for the questions was as tricky as possible, turning on the most minuscule facts and figures. It was not so much a test to see how much chemistry a student knew; it was more like a test to see how well a student could read Mr. Kistler's mind and outmaneuver him.

Even for Amber, Kistler's mid term was a bear. Without the lab equipment in the way, though, she could focus on the test, instead of focusing on Jake's wandering, cheating eyes. She flew through the test without a single thought except for the correct answer to each question.

Amber finished her mid term with time to spare. There were a few questions that she felt unsure about. But she could feel that her grade would be a good one. She closed her eyes for a moment to relax. Her status on the swim team was safe. Her world was right. She had trusted God, and it had paid off.

After mentally whispering a quick prayer of thanks, she turned over her paper to read through the answers one more time. Kistler was such a master at stating a seemingly obvious question but changing one word that would trip you up. She set out looking for that one word in every question.

Her gaze ran up and down the pages of answers. There! She found one. She furiously erased her answer and started over. Unfortunately, she let her guard down. She didn't notice Jake raising up off his lab stool to get a glance at her paper.

"*Miss Thomas,* bring your test here immediately," Mr. Kistler said sharply, looking down his nose through his bifocals.

His voice startled Amber so much that she dropped her pencil. As she looked up, though, she caught sight of Jake, working a little too hard at being casual. In an instant, she knew that, once again, he had found a way to ruin a perfectly good moment. Amber carried her paper up to the desk at the front of the room.

Mr. Kistler pulled her over to the corner. He stood over her with his back to the class and half-whispered, half-whined, "Amber, had it not been for your odd behavior these last few weeks, I never would have believed that you would cheat on an examination. Nevertheless, just now I witnessed you sharing answers with Jake Smith, and I want an explanation."

Amber felt tongue-tied. She had worked so hard to trust God and not worry. She wasn't ready for this to blow up in her face. "I was not, *not* giving Jake answers," she finally stammered.

The next thing she knew Mr. Kistler motioned to Jake and he joined their huddle. Jake put on his "what?" face. Playing dumb only created a worse chemical reaction in the teacher. "I have no choice," Mr. Kistler said, his voice rising. "School policy says you both get an F." Deliberately, he wrote two big, fat F's on their papers. The ink was as red as his face. Scarlet letters. Amber had never gotten an F before.

"Please, Mr. Kistler," Amber began.

But she couldn't go on. Her teacher held up his hand to stop. "Tell it to the principal. Now!"

Once they were in the hall, Amber's tongue untied itself and she exploded. "Now look what you've done! This means I'm off the swim team. I'm going to let the whole team down, and it's *your* fault, Jake."

"My fault?" Jake stopped and faced Amber. "Who's been turning in quizzes unfinished? You lowered your own grades, Amber. All I was doing was asking for a little help. But oh, no. You are way too high and mighty to actually give me a hand up." Jake stormed off down the hall ahead of her.

"Oh no you don't," said Amber, grabbing his arm and pulling him back. "I'm not the one who cheated, Jake. You put me in a horrible position. I have helped you out in the past, but this was asking too much. I'll tell you this—you better find it in your heart to clear this up with Mr. Kistler, and you had better do it quick, or . . . I don't know what I'll do. But I'll find a way to make you sorry for this."

"Oh, so you're threatening me?" Jake fired back. "You think I'm going to be scared? You were frightened by a stupid e-mail threat, Amber. Remember? You'll get yours? Well, you got *yours*, Amber. And the way I look at it, you took me down with you. Would it have been so impossible for you to let my life be a little easier? All I needed was a break in chemistry. You couldn't even give me that."

Jake stalked off, leaving Amber trembling in the hallway. She had put on a good show of anger for him. But what she really felt was hurt—hurt and disappointed. Hadn't she trusted God? Was this what success felt like? She had tried to please everyone and had ended up letting everyone down, including herself. Maybe Jake was right. Would it have been such a big deal to help him?

Amber walked slowly the rest of the way to the office. She didn't even want to breathe the same air as Jake until she had to. She turned the last corner and looked through the wall of glass that separated the secretary's office from the hallway. Jake was sitting in one of the squeaky fake-leather chairs with his face in his hands.

Amber's heart broke for both of them. She wanted to help, but she was having a hard time helping herself. How could she help her friend? And why did she feel like he was her friend when he was giving her such a hard time? She had to wonder how people got inside of your heart that way.

She was still angry, though. And she was almost as angry at Jake as she was at herself. Amber entered the room silently and sat across from Jake, staring into space. The war between them was over. They had both lost.

chapter.13

Amber followed Coach to the pool area. The last thing she wanted to do was to see the teammates she'd let down. Word had traveled fast that Amber was off the swim team for now. Coach hadn't said much to her. But when she had gone to her locker after last period, he had been waiting for her. When he asked her to pick up her things in the locker room, she could hardly refuse—not after what she'd done to his team.

Swimmers were clustered around the bulletin board as Amber tried to sneak past to the locker room. Instead of the usual excited chatter over who was listed for what, there were only quiet whisperings and one very loud freshman voice.

"I have to swim backstroke? Why should I have to change because Amber can't keep her act together?"

Amber knew that meant Coach had assigned Alex to take her

place in backstroke for the relay. Tess, a sophomore, would take Alex's freestyle spot.

Coach spoke matter-of-factly. "With Amber out of the pool, Alex is the fastest we've got on back. I hate to pull you off of free for the medley, Alex, but you still have it for individuals. It's what we call a contingency plan. It's making the best of what we have available. Now, go suit up, and let's get some yards in."

Amber hurried into the locker room. Seconds later, she heard Alex and Morgan come in. Amber ducked behind a row of lockers so they wouldn't see her.

"It's not fair, Morgan," Alex complained. "Now I'm going to look like the reason we lose. And we *are* going to lose."

"Everyone knows it's not your fault, Alex," Morgan said. "You're a terrific swimmer. Everybody knows that. So calm down, and just give it your best. We'll be behind you."

"I know I'm an outsider coming in," Alex griped. "But I thought if I could help the team win, then maybe I wouldn't have to feel so out of place anymore. Now it's going to be worse than ever. I know what my best is in freestyle. I don't even know my time in backstroke. If I blow the race, I don't want to get blamed for something that's Amber's deal."

The girls moved out of earshot then, but Amber stayed until she heard them leave. *Funny,* she thought, *I got in this mess because I tried to keep everyone happy. Now I'm letting everyone down. This can't get any worse.*

She listened as the girls in the next room got ready for practice. She heard them pad out to the pool one by one. Everything she had worked so hard to keep—her team's success, her friends' approval, her good grades—all those things were gone. And she was left with a weary spirit and lot of confusion where her trust in God had been.

Amber sat quietly in her misery and listened until there was no one left in the locker room. She closed the door separating the junk room from the lockers and sat in the dark. When she finally couldn't take it anymore, she put her head in her arms and cried as hard as she had ever cried in her life.

When Amber got home from school, her face was raw from the cold wind drying the last traces of her tears. She sat at her desk and stared out the window. She couldn't make sense of everything. She had done what was right. She had trusted God. But life had not turned out well. What should she have done differently? Where was the happy ending?

Without even thinking she reached over and flipped the switch on her computer. As it whirred through its warmups, she closed her eyes and felt one more tear slide down her face. *I can't believe I have any left*, she thought. Her eyes felt puffy. Her cheeks were sore from wiping away the tears in case someone caught her crying. She laid her head against the back of the chair and took a few deep breaths.

When she opened her eyes, she clicked to the list of favorite places in her Web browser and heard the modem connect to

TodaysGirls.com. Before she could react, her Thought for the Day popped up on the screen.

Trust the Lord with all your heart.
Are your plans falling apart? Are your best-laid plans making things worse rather than better? Trust God to bring it all together in the end.

But I did trust God, and look where it got me, Amber thought. *My teacher thinks I'm a liar, and my team is going to compete without me. Now my parents are going to find out, and who knows what they'll think. How can God bring it all together in the end? This is the end, isn't it?*

Amber alt-tabbed over to her Bible program and called up the last screen to see her mom's favorite verse again.

Trust the Lord with all your heart.
Don't depend on your own understanding.
Remember the Lord in everything you do.
And he will give you success.

PROVERBS 3:5–6

She prayed silently, "God, it sure looks like things are worse than they were when I was handling things myself. I guess all I can do is to keep trusting you, remembering you in everything

I do. Please show me what to do next. It feels like my heart is breaking. Amen."

She flipped back over to the Web site and entered the chat room. Maya was the only one already in the room.

faithful1: hello?

nycbutterfly: hi. I was hoping u'd come by.

faithful1: I'm glad you're 'talking' to me.

nycbutterfly: I just got home from practice. I wanted to call but didn't know if u'd want to hear from me.

faithful1: I'll always want to hear from u, even when we're fighting.

nycbutterfly: I'm thinking u must feel pretty bummed about now.

faithful1: I'd say bummed is a good word to describe it.

nycbutterfly: What happened? I heard you and Jake were caught cheating and got Fs. Anybody who knows YOU knows that isn't true. What's wrong with that man?

faithful1: Which man? Jake or Kistler?

nycbutterfly: we know Jake is an out of control jerk and I wouldn't call him a man. I'm talking about Kistler.

faithful1: Mr. Kistler wouldn't believe me. He wouldn't even listen. He's so out of touch with anything except his own red marker and grade book. Jake just played it off like we were in it together. He's a pro. He ought to go to Hollywood. He could play a great villain.

nycbutterfly: I can't believe that Jake Smith. Rotten . . . Have your parents said anything yet?

faithful1: no. I'm wondering if I should go ahead and tell them or just let them hear from the school. Either way I hate it. Somebody might have already called them by now.

nycbutterfly: I'm sorry I walked away the other day. I really do care more about you than about winning the medley. What can I do 4 u?

faithful1: I don't think there's anything to do, nyc. Thanx. One thing I've learned from this is to ask for help a lot sooner. I thought I could handle it on my own, but it would have been better if I had gone to my parents or to Coach and let them help. I just didn't want to seem like a kid, u know?

nycbutterfly: I'm glad you see that now. Sometimes you just try to do 2 much on your own. It's OK to let people help you. You certainly do your share for everybody else.

faithful1: That's part of what confused me. Maybe I should have helped Jake. Maybe it was partly my own selfishness that caused this. If I hadn't left those quizzes unfinished in the first place I wouldn't have been put on probation. Maybe you were right. Maybe

I should have just let him cheat and helped him out.

nycbutterfly: Do u really think that would have helped him?

faithful1: it would have helped him get better grades.

nycbutterfly: But, do u really think that would have helped him?

faithful1: u already said that.

nycbutterfly: Yeah, but u never answered it. What kind of help do u want to be? Do you want to help people get good grades or be better people?

faithful1: hey wait a minit!! u were the one telling me to let him cheat

nycbutterfly: Yes, I was. But I didn't say that because I wanted u to HELP Jake. I was just mad and scared about the meet. U're talking about helping someone by doing something you know is wrong. That doesn't make sense to me.

faithful1: I see what u're saying. I guess I've just been trying to make sense out of it. I wish I had depended on God to help me know what to do. I wonder how differently this all would have ended up if I had done that.

nycbutterfly: How do u think God would have helped?

faithful1: I don't know what he would have done, but I think he would have shown me SOMETHING if I had even asked. I waited until everything became a mess before I even prayed about it all.

nycbutterfly: so u think God may have helped you not make a mess, but you don't think he'll help you clean up one?

faithful1: hmmmmm . . .

nycbutterfly: oh yeah. 1 more thing. What were you THINKING trashing Coach's yard Friday night? Did he get you back or what?

faithful1: We didn't trash it, not really. We just added a bit of fall décor. But u're right. He got us back 4sure.

nycbutterfly: I'm glad I wasn't in on that one.

faithful1: we'll do it again sometime if u r feeling left out.

nycbutterfly: no thanx. Oops, gotta go. Alex's over here to study with Morgan. I think I'll go work in my room for a while. I'll talk to u tomorrow. Good luck with the parents.

faithful1: Thanx. It's really good to talk to you. Thank you.

faithful1 left the room

nycbutterfly left the room

chapter.14

Tuesday morning, Amber sat again in the waiting area outside of the principal's office. It always surprised her that this room had almost an antiseptic smell. The only reason Amber could figure for that was the closet behind the secretary's desk that held her secret cleaning supplies. The secretary was a little over the top about germs. Since most of the chairs were that fake leather stuff, Amber figured she probably wiped them down after every person left.

For the last few minutes, Amber had been mentally reviewing the facts of her case. She had thought through the quizzes, the studying, and the midterm. Each little part by itself had not seemed like a big deal. But put them all together . . .

"That's how choices work," her dad had said. "They pile up on top of you after a while. That's why it's better to make the

little choices really well, so the big ones will come more natu-
rally." That was just part of his sermon from the night before,
when she told her parents about why they had been invited to
the school. She had been honest with them. She even told them
it was Jake, the son of her dad's golfing buddy. Dad almost
choked on that one.

Her parents responded typically for them. Her dad paced
around the den and tried to figure out a way to fix things. Her
mom cried and tried to help her feel better. To their credit, they
didn't doubt her word at all. They believed that she had done
her best to keep Jake from cheating. But they also reminded her
that she should have come to them earlier.

The only thing she hadn't told them about was the Stranger. Today, sitting on the high school equivalent of death row,
she thought that keeping that secret might have been a mistake. The Stranger had played a bigger role in all this than she
had given him credit for. After all, if she hadn't been
so scared of Jake potentially being the Stranger, maybe she
would have stood up to him sooner. Whoever the Stranger
was, he had made her life miserable and filled her with fear.
That fear pushed her even farther away from making good
choices.

So far, this morning had been a waiting game. First, her par-
ents and Jake's mom met with Kistler and the principal, Ms.
Clark. That left Jake and Amber alone. Amber hadn't talked to
Jake. She hadn't even looked at him. For once in his life, he left

her alone as well. It had been a relief when Ms. Clark had called Jake in first. Now Amber was ready to go in, take her medicine, and be done with this whole process.

"Amber, you can come in now." Amber hadn't even heard the door open, but she bolted out of her chair and toward the door Ms. Clark was holding open for her. Finally, an end in sight.

Ms. Clark looked past Amber and said, "You might as well step inside for a moment, too." Amber turned around to see Coach Short standing by the teachers' mailboxes. He looked as surprised as Amber, but he did as he was told. Most everyone at the school responded to Ms. Clark that way.

Amber's parents smiled solemnly as she walked into the room. She sat down beside her dad. Jake was sitting next to his mom. He didn't look up.

Mr. Kistler was the first one to speak. "Amber, some things have changed since the last time we talked. Jake has shared some new information with us today that may change the status on the swim meet this afternoon. That is, if you can corroborate his story."

Amber glanced at Jake. He stared at his shoes as if he were watching a video game. There was no telling what he thought Mr. Kistler was asking her to do. If Mr. Kistler wanted her to confirm Jake's story, the real question was what story Jake wanted her to confirm.

Mr. Kistler continued. "Jake tells us that he has been attempting to cheat off of your quizzes for quite some time. He says that when you failed to complete the last several quizzes, it was in an attempt to keep him from cheating. Is this true?"

Amber looked at Jake again. She wondered why he was suddenly being so up-front. "Yes, sir. That's true. I thought if I just stopped giving him answers, he would leave me alone."

"And on the day of the midterm examination," Mr. Kistler said, "did you allow him to copy your answers?"

"I tried to ignore him, Mr. Kistler. My mom had told me about this Bible verse that said if I trusted in God, he would make my paths straight. I felt like the straightest path for me was to be honest and to do well on the test, and to leave Jake up to his own conscience. I wasn't going to leave my midterm unfinished. But I didn't think Jake saw my answers at all during the test. But, then, as I rechecked my answers, I relaxed, and he must have been able to see my paper. That's when you saw us and thought I was showing him my answers."

Amber could feel her mother looking at her. *Please don't cry here.*

Ms. Clark took control. "Amber, there is something about this whole situation that puzzles me. From everything I've observed in you, you are a strong, smart, assertive young woman. I know that you have a history with Jake because your families are friends. Still, I have a sense that there is more here than I've been told. Is there something you could share with us to help us understand why this situation has spiraled so far out of control?"

"Well, I did wonder if I was being a real friend to Jake by not letting him cheat. We always hear about how we're supposed to help each other out and how we're supposed to turn the other cheek. Maybe if I hadn't worried about it so much during the quizzes—"

Ms. Clark broke into the conversation. "Amber, let me stop you right there. Letting Jake steal answers from you would not be helping him. He doesn't need that kind of friendship. If you had let him cheat, you would have taken away his chance to excel and to learn. You would have taken from him rather than helped him. Do you understand that?"

"I'm beginning to," Amber answered. "In fact a friend told me just about that same thing yesterday."

"Is there anything else, Amber?"

Amber took a big breath. It was time for the Stranger to come out of the closet. She only hoped she wasn't about to get Jake in even more trouble. "There is something that I haven't shared with anyone here. But this morning I realized that it's a big piece of the puzzle for me.

"Last Thursday, the night before that last chemistry quiz, I received a somewhat threatening e-mail on a secure site. At least, I thought it was secure." Amber could feel six pairs of concerned adult eyes (including one pair of beady adult eyes) bear down on her. "I assumed, and I still think it's a possibility, that the e-mail came from Jake, under the name Stranger, to intimidate me into letting him cheat off of my quizzes. I got scared, and I think that fear caused me to close up even more from the people who could have helped me."

Amber watched all stares shift from her to Jake. With this kind of pressure, she felt sure that she would finally know if Jake was the Stranger or not.

Ms. Clark spoke first. "Jake? Help us out here. Have you been threatening Amber over the Internet?"

Jake looked around at everyone in the room. "No, I have not. I told her that when Maya showed me the message. I don't even have access to a computer. Ask my parents."

"He's telling you the truth," said Mrs. Smith. "Our computer has been down for months, and we haven't had the money to get it fixed. I don't think Jake had the opportunity to threaten Amber. He surely wouldn't have the technology to break his way into a secure site."

"I'm telling the truth!" said Jake. "Okay, so that doesn't mean much anymore. Look, I cheated on some schoolwork. I know that's wrong, and I feel *certain* I'll be punished for it. But I'm not going to play some cloak-and-dagger game with one of the few real friends I have. I did *not* threaten Amber. I am *not* the Stranger."

Jake's mom looked relieved. At least her son was off the hook on one count. Amber's parents, if anything, looked more worried. If Jake wasn't the Stranger, who was? A real stranger was threatening their child. Coach looked about as solemn as Amber had ever seen him.

"Amber," Mr. Kistler resumed, "it seems to me that the grade you made on the midterm was a fair grade. Not only that, it was a good grade: a 99. I understand from the coach that you have a very important contest in a few hours. I'm sure your parents will want to talk with you more about this, but at this point I'm removing your academic probation. If your parents and your coach are agreed, you can compete this afternoon."

I can compete! Amber thought. She knew what Coach would have to say about it, so she looked at her parents, hoping, hoping, and hoping . . .

Her dad spoke first, and not to her. "Coach, if Amber competes this afternoon, when will she need to be there?"

"The same as usual," said Coach. "The girls need to be at the pool suited up no later than five o'clock. Amber might want to come early and put in some extra laps since she's missed a couple of practices, but I don't think it will be a problem."

Amber's dad looked at her mom. Amber held her breath as Mom nodded. "Fine," Mom said at last.

Her dad turned to Coach. "We'll have her there then."

Amber knew that she was in for hours of lectures and fatherly explanations from her dad and more hours of probing and counseling from her mom. Still, she was on! They were letting her swim!

Principal Clark spoke up. "You all are free to go. I know you have a lot to talk about. Thank you for taking the time to meet as we sorted out the facts. Please let me know how I can assist you in the future. Mr. and Mrs. Thomas, I have some errands to run. You are free to use my office if you need a place to talk with Amber for a few minutes."

"Thank you. We'll do that," Mrs. Thomas said. Then she turned to Jake. "And thank you, Jake, for telling the truth. I know that must have been difficult. Tell your dad 'hello' for us, and I hope he's feeling better soon."

Jake didn't say anything. He just looked at the floor.

With a quick thumbs-up, Coach Short practically skipped out of the room toward the gym.

chapter.15

When Amber walked into the pool area, everyone cheered. Coach had already filled them in, and Bren had Amber's suit ready. But the last person she expected to see was standing right inside the door—Jake Smith.

"Hi, Amber."

"Hi, Jake. Thanks for speaking up."

"I didn't really want to, but I'm kinda glad now that I did."

"Why *did* you tell the truth finally, Jake?"

"It was that letter Mr. Kistler sent home to our parents. After my dad got it, he forced the whole story out of me."

"Yeah, my parents hit the roof. I didn't want to tell them it was you. Our dads have been friends a long time, and I didn't want—"

"I know. Everything was a mess. I was out of control. Anyway, I just wanted to tell you that I'm sorry, and that I was telling the truth when I said I wasn't your evil e-mailer. Good luck at the meet!"

"Thanks, Jake. Good luck with your parents." Amber watched Jake walk out the doors and found herself wishing that he *was* the Stranger. At least everything would be solved then. She was so excited to be swimming, though, that the Stranger would just have to wait.

"Amber, come on!" Maya called. "Let's go!"

Amber jogged over to the locker room and smiled at her teammates. They chanted together, "We're gonna win! We're gonna win! Amber wondered though. She'd had so many distractions. Could she could pull off her leg of the relay? *There's no time to worry now,* she thought. *I'll just have to give it my best shot and see what happens. At least it's just a straight path down the pool and back. That's one straight path in my life that I can't lose sight of.*

When Amber dived into the water, she felt like she'd just gotten home from a long trip. She rolled onto her back and started down the length of the pool. The flags flying above her were like old friends waving a hello and cheering her on.

At the other end of the pool she rested her hand on the grainy edge, closed her eyes, and lay back, suspended in the water. From the time when she was too small to touch in the shallow end, Amber had loved floating. Never was she more relaxed than when she emptied all tension and let the water hold her in a long, numbing float.

"Hi there!" an unfamiliar voice shouted above her. She opened her eyes to see someone standing beside the pool looking down at her. The light was behind him so she could only make out his shape. It was a man's voice, deep and gravelly.

Amber pushed her swim goggles up on her forehead. With one hand she shielded her eyes in the hope of seeing the face of whoever-this-was.

"You're Amber, right?" he asked.

She nodded, then looked around to find that she was the only swimmer at that end of the pool. "Who are you?" she asked.

"You don't know me, but I'm a fan of yours," he said. Amber squinted, but she still couldn't make out his face because of the lights. His voice sounded about as old as Coach's. "I'm looking forward to watching you swim today. I've been watching all season, actually. You're quite good."

A shrill whistle sounded and Amber's head snapped around to see Coach waving to her from the other end of the pool. "I gotta go," said Amber. *This is him!* she wanted to yell out.

"Sure thing, Amber. Talk to you later. Don't be a stranger!" Amber's heart was beating hard as she swam down to the other end of the pool.

"Who was that, Amber?" Coach asked her as soon as she got out of the water.

"I'm not sure," she said honestly. "He must come to a lot of the meets. Do you recognize him?"

"I thought I'd seen him before," he answered. "But don't go wandering off, OK? Let's be cautious, Amber."

Another day Amber might have told the coach he worried too much. Not today. She looked over to see where the "fan" was seated. He smiled and waved.

Soon it was time for the meet to begin. The jam boxes were turned off, and the clocks started. In what seemed like just a few more minutes, the announcer called for the 200-medley relay. It was time for the girls to pull together as a team.

Amber, Maya, Morgan, and Alex gathered around Coach. "OK, girls," he said. "We've been through a lot in the last week. Let's put it all out of our minds. Just swim. You're our best. Work together as a team, and you can come in first. Let's do it!"

Coach put his right hand out. Amber placed her right hand on his, and the others followed suit. "Go team!" they shouted and headed for lane three.

Amber was up first. Swimming backstroke, she would start in the water instead of diving off the block. She jumped in the water and positioned herself against the end of the pool. Her hands felt the familiar rough edges above the smooth tiles. Her feet were flat against the wall, ready to push with every bit of strength she had.

The air felt electric as Amber waited for the starting gun. Every second, every breath, every muscle mattered. In this kind of contest, seconds made the difference. There were two other teams, including Baldwin, with times equal to Edgewood's. That meant Amber's team would have to fight for every stroke to get ahead.

Amber heard the ref say, "Take your mark!" Everything around her faded to stillness. It was like that at every meet. *So far, so good,* she thought.

Bang!

She pushed against the wall with everything inside her. Then she threw back her arms and arched her back. She sliced through the water in full-motion. Hers was the first leg of the race. It was her role to put her team as far ahead as she possibly could by the time Morgan entered the water.

Amber gauged her distance by the familiar flags above her. *Closer to the wall . . . Near the wall . . . and . . . turn!* She did a backflip at just the right time and pushed off once again to head back toward the touch pad at the other end of the pool. By the time she surfaced, she was on her back again. Her arms worked together like a powerful machine propelling her to the other end, where her teammates were cheering.

Amber swam as if she were going to ram right into the wall. Just as she felt the familiar tile, she saw Morgan over her head, diving into the water for her leg of the breaststroke. When she pulled out of the water, Amber saw that she'd beaten Baldwin's swimmer in lane two, but just barely. Lane four came in third.

Morgan swam like a frog on fire. Her head bobbed up and

down the length of the pool. Lane two pulled a little ahead of her just after the turn. By the time Morgan was halfway across the pool, though, she had closed the gap and was gaining.

Amber had pulled herself out of the pool and stood with her teammates, calling out Morgan's name as if that would bring her to their side of the pool sooner. For Amber, the pressure was off. As she watched Morgan's progress she caught sight of the "fan" she had met earlier. He gave her a thumbs-up sign and smiled. Amber pretended she didn't see him.

When Maya sailed off the starting block, she was as graceful as she was powerful. She and the Baldwin swimmer in lane two looked synchronized. Stroke for stroke, they fought their way down the pool. After the turn, though, the swimmer in lane two burst ahead. By the time Maya neared the wall, Baldwin's free-style swimmer was already in the water.

"Go, go, go!" Amber yelled as Alex finally got to dive in. Amber allowed her eyes to scan the crowd. The man in the blue jacket had moved. She spotted him halfway down the side of the pool, watching Alex swim her heart out.

Alex had started out behind, but it didn't seem to bother her. She swam as if she were swimming for her life, as if this victory meant everything to her.

At the turn, Alex had closed the Baldwin gap by half. Amber had never seen anyone swim like Alex was swimming. The phrase "reckless abandon" came to her mind.

Halfway down the pool, Alex was almost even with lane two

and still picking up speed. The crowd screamed. Fans rose to their feet. Shouts echoed off the walls and water.

Ten meters . . . five meters . . . and the two swimmers slapped the touch pad. Loudspeakers announced the official victory: "Edgewood by less than a second!"

The whole relay team pulled Alex out of the water and grabbed her for a group hug. Coach Short was smiling all over himself.

When the hug broke up and the swimmers for the next race moved into place, Amber looked around to find Maya. Instead, she saw the unfamiliar fan walking toward her. She could see his face clearly, and in that moment felt sure that he was not someone she wanted to get to know. Out of the corner of her eye she saw Coach moving in to cut off the man before he got to the team.

Someone grabbed Amber's arm. "We did it!" Maya whooped.

"Maya!" Amber yelled. "I think that man is the Stranger!" She could barely hear above the tangle of teams shouting back and forth, changing places all at once. She pointed the man out to Maya, just as he reached inside his jacket. "No!" Amber yelled.

"Amber! Who? What?" Maya yelled back. The speaker blared with the names of winners and losers.

"The Stranger! That's him! The *e-mail.*" Amber kept her gaze locked on Coach's back.

Maya's eyes got wide. "Amber! He's the Stranger? Are you sure?"

Amber couldn't see the Stranger. "We have to get closer!" she shouted, pulling Maya with her. They moved in until she could see the Stranger's face.

"Coach sure doesn't look scared," Maya said.

She was right. To Amber's amazement, Coach was smiling and talking calmly. The blue-coated man held a pad of paper in his hand and was writing as fast as he could. Maya and Amber crept closer as the man shook Coach's hand.

"Thank you so much, Coach Short. You'll see the write-up in tomorrow's newspaper. Tell the team to look for it." Before he walked away he waved at Amber and Maya. "Great swim!"

Coach rolled his eyes at them. "You had me ready to punch out the sports editor for the *Edgewood Times*. What would he have written about us in the paper then?"

chapter.16

Amber had to laugh, watching Coach try to stop smiling. But he had a lot to smile about. His team had broken several of their best times. They came in first in three major categories including the medley relay. What more could a coach ask for? As the girls paraded to the locker room, Coach shook each hand and congratulated them all over again.

Inside the locker room were wall-to-wall smiles. Even the conversations sounded happier, almost like music. Swimmers grinned as they shoved each other at the dryers. Laughter poured out of shower stalls.

Alex didn't even complain when she had to wait her turn in the locker room. Amber actually caught her dancing on the benches, using a towel for a microphone and singing a song about dancing all night long. Besides pulling out a win for the relay team, she had placed first in the 50-meter freestyle and the 200-meter freestyle.

When there were just a few girls left in the locker room, Amber joined Alex at the mirror. While Alex tried to get a comb through her curls, Amber put on lip gloss. "Great swim today, huh?" she said, leaning into the mirror and covering her lips with strawberry gloss. The strong strawberry scent made her hungry.

"I'd say it was great!" answered Alex, switching to a brush for the tangles.

Amber didn't think she'd ever seen Alex in such a good mood. In fact, she'd never seen the girl smile. She was pretty when she smiled. Amber wished she'd seen this side of Alex before. "You really made your mark today, Alex."

Alex turned to Amber and acted like she wanted to tell her something. "Amber—"

"Hey, everybody!" Maya called out. "Look what the dog dragged in. It's a Jamie!"

Jamie flashed a huge smile. "I didn't know until I got here that Amber was going to swim. I'm so happy for you guys. You looked like pros out there."

"That's 'cause we *are* pros!" shouted Alex.

"Please excuse our mascot. We call her 'the ego,'" said Maya. "She carries the pride around for all of us."

"If so, I guess we'll have to invite her to the Gnosh for a post-meet celebration. The mascot has to be a part, doesn't she?" asked Jamie.

Amber glanced over at Maya. Maya shrugged. "How about it, Alex?" Amber asked.

Alex looked doubtful. "I don't know. I might have other things to do, you know?"

"Alex," Morgan said in a warning kind of mother tone. "We want you to come. Don't be difficult."

Alex turned from the mirror and faced the girls. "Since you asked nicely, I guess I'll go." She turned back to the mirror, and Maya rolled her eyes at Amber.

As Amber walked away, she heard Alex mutter, "Guess I'm no stranger now, huh?"

Amber jerked her head around. "What did you say?"

Alex stared down at her comb. She hesitated before answering. "I didn't say anything."

"Oh, yes, you did," said Maya, walking up behind Alex. "You said you're not a stranger now. What did you mean by that?"

Alex shrank back against the mirror as the girls circled her. "I didn't mean anything. I just meant that I'm not a new kid anymore and . . ."

"It was you, wasn't it?" Morgan whispered. "All this time I've been defending you, and it was you who sent those e-mails."

Alex's face hardened. But her voice came out as squeaky as Bren's marshmallow puppet. "What e-mails?"

"You mean you're the one who's been terrorizing Amber this whole stinking time?" Jamie screamed.

Part of Amber wanted to shake Alex until her head bobbed

like a clown's. But the other part wanted to hug her for being a brat instead of a danger. Instead, she grabbed Alex's arm. "There's only one way we can handle this. Maya turn on the shower."

"Cold only?" Maya asked.

"You guys!" Morgan begged.

"Cold only," Jamie answered for Amber.

Jamie took Alex's other arm as she and Amber dragged Alex into the showers. Maya had the cold water running full-blast. Morgan trailed behind them calling out, "It'll be over before you know it, Alex!" But Morgan didn't attempt a rescue. Every swimmer in the locker room knew what was coming, and they'd all lived through it.

Before Alex could put up much of a struggle, Amber, Jamie, and Maya were holding her under the icy cold shower. At first, Alex accepted her fate, but not for long. The second Amber loosened her grip, Alex pulled her into the shower.

Amber's feet slipped on the shower floor. Maya reached out to catch her. But as soon as Maya let go of Alex's arm, Alex reached up to the shower nozzle and twisted it around to spray the other girls.

Jamie pulled back the curtain to the next shower and aimed that nozzle at Alex. Within minutes, they were all soaking wet, laughing and screaming. Before it was over, they were strewn like wet towels all over the locker room floor.

Morgan turned off the showers, and the girls surveyed the

damage. The entire shower area looked like a monsoon had passed through.

"Yoo-hoo! Anybody here?" Bren's voice filtered through the locker room and into the showers.

"Bring us some towels!" called Amber.

"OK," Bren said. She turned the corner into the showers and stopped. "I'm thinking we've got a story to tell?" she asked, raising her eyebrows.

"Bren, meet the Stranger," Jamie said.

The dripping wet Alex got to her feet and grinned sheepishly.

"You mean," Bren said slowly, "this little wet munchkin is the one who caused all that trouble?" She threw a towel at Alex. "What are you going to do about it, Amber?" she demanded.

Amber took a towel from Bren. "Consider it handled," she said, grinning at Bren and Alex.

Bren passed around towels to the rest of the girls. "I'm going to the Gnosh with you guys, but I'm not going with you looking like this, so let the reconstruction begin, and soon."

chapter.17

"You're a brat," Amber told Alex as they dried their hair in front of the mirror. "You know that, don't you?" Most of her anger had gone down the drain with the water fight.

"It was just a joke," Alex replied. "I didn't mean to wreck your life or anything. My grandma has an old computer. I sent the e-mails before I left for swim practice in the morning."

Amber raised an eyebrow. "That's how they got there so early. You really had me going, Alex."

"I didn't realize all the other stuff that was happening too," Alex asked.

"But how did you get my password?" Amber asked.

Alex smiled. "The first time we got our gym bags mixed up I saw your password and address in a folder inside your bag. I didn't look at anything else in there, though. I promise."

Amber shook her head as all the pieces fell into place. She gathered her stuff and headed toward the locker room door.

"Amber?"

She turned to see Alex walking toward her with a gym bag.

"Oh, no," said Amber good-naturedly, "did I pick up *your* bag this time?"

"No," Alex said quietly. "I've got mine. I just wanted to say I'm . . ." Alex paused and looked down.

"You're . . . ?" prompted Amber.

"Well, I'm . . . really impressed with the way you swam today. You got us off to a great start."

"Thanks, Alex. You made all the difference, bringing us home. See you at the Gnosh." Amber started walking again.

Alex reached out and touched Amber's arm. "One more thing, Amber, I just wanted to say I'm . . ."

"What is it, Alex? I've got to go. My parents are still hanging out to see me."

"I'm really sorry about everything."

Amber could tell that apologies were not one of Alex's favorite things. "Thanks for saying that, Alex. I know you didn't know everything that was going on. There's no way you could have known what the e-mail would have meant to me. We're OK."

Alex relaxed. "Thanks."

Amber grinned at Alex and got a true smile in return. "Of course, we still might have to have a talk about the seats in the van."

Amber turned to go. Then she got an idea. "Hey, why don't you sign on tonight in the TodaysGirls.com chat room. Walk out with me, and we'll talk about your screen name."

At the Gnosh Pit, Jamie had already decorated the winners' table (one of the round booths in the back corner) with streamers. By the time Amber and her teammates got there, so many fans from Edgewood had stopped by that the whole place broke out in applause.

Bren did her parade-wave to the room. Maya clasped her hands over her head as a conquering hero, and Alex took a bow. Amber and Morgan tried to get to their table, but it took them almost ten minutes to make their way to the back.

The girls crowded into the booth and ordered their favorites. Chicken tenders for Morgan. Onion rings for Bren. A burger for Alex. A grilled chicken sandwich for Amber. Grilled cheese for Jamie. A club sandwich for Maya. Before long they were munching and sipping and recounting Amber's almost-experience with the would-be Stranger. With each retelling, the story got longer, and the Stranger got more sinister.

"Remember that guy in the blue coat?" Maya could barely get it out; she was laughing so hard. "You were terrified of him, Amber!"

Amber was laughing just as hard at herself. "What was scary was when he reached into his pocket while he was talking to Coach. You know what I was thinking?"

Maya's laugh died out. "Yeah. Me too."

"Yeah," Bren agreed. "Pens! Pens can be sooooo dangerous!" she teased. "Mightier than the sword and all. I thought he might *write* so many words he would hurt Coach, didn't you, Alex?"

Alex grinned. She looked happier than Amber had ever seen her. She liked that Bren was including Alex in the joke. "Did you see how Coach smiled after giving the guy the interview? I bet he'll have the article posted on every bulletin board at school."

"All two inches of it!" said Bren.

"It's funny how sometimes life works out the right way, just when you think it's not going to," Amber said, chewing on a fry.

"Oh, she's going to get philosophical now after saving the world from a small-town reporter," Bren warned.

"No, I am *not*. I'm just saying, there are so many things that can go wrong in life. Days like today are something to feel grateful about." Amber held back a yawn. "Maybe I *am* getting philosophical. I'm putting myself to sleep!"

Amber's parents walked by the girls' table. "Hi there!" Dad said. "I see the winning team is all here. We're on our way out."

"Great swim, girls!" Mom said.

Amber's dad picked up his daughter's bill from the table. "Tell you what. You shouldn't have to buy your own celebration dinner. Pass those bills right this way."

"Thanks, Mr. and Mrs. Thomas!" Morgan cried. The others agreed, and the rest of the scribbled sheets of dinner orders found their way to Amber's dad.

"See you at home soon, though, huh, Amber?"

"I'll be right behind you," Amber agreed. "I'm beat."

After Amber's parents had gone, Amber sighed. "Now I can finally sleep with my computer plugged in again."

Maya lowered her glass in mid-swallow. "What?!"

"Wait until you hear this one," added Jamie.

Amber couldn't get her words out right, as she thought about her images of the Stranger, who was only Alex, coming through her computer cables. "I thought—" But she burst into another laughing fit and couldn't finish.

"I know why," Jamie said. But she fell into the same laughter, and couldn't explain either.

Bren started laughing just because they were. Alex and Morgan giggled at Bren when she laughed so hard she snorted.

Maya stared at them like they were all crazy. She tried to get them to calm down enough so they could explain what they were laughing at. Finally, she slammed her glass down on the table. "Order!" she shouted. "I demand order in the Gnosh!"

Gasping for air, Amber put one hand to her chest. "Let me explain," she pleaded as she tried to catch her breath. "I was getting really freaked out about these e-mails. Sorry, Alex. It's like I got this image of the Stranger coming at me through the computer cable. One night after I climbed in bed, I got all uptight about it and unplugged the thing. I've . . . been doing it . . . ever since!" she choked out, as she fell into gales of laughter again.

Bren stared at Amber in amazement. "What did you think would happen, brain-o? Did you think the Stranger would float out like dust and get you?"

"Like a genie!" added Morgan.

"Like a ghost!" chimed in Alex.

Bren reached over and lifted Alex's thick hair until it stood out from her head. "Can't you see this coming through the cables at you in the middle of the night?"

Alex pushed Bren away, but grinned at Morgan.

"It just goes to show you what fear does," Amber said. "It makes you a little crazy in the head."

Maya and Jamie were still shaking their heads in disbelief.

"Anyway," said Amber, "it's all behind us. With all the work at the beginning, I should've known the site was safe. Let's get out of here for now, but let's chat before we go to bed tonight."

Bren frowned. "Do you think that's possible, Amber?"

"What do you mean? Is something wrong with the site?"

"No. But to sign on, you'll have to plug the computer in, and I wouldn't want to put you in any danger." Bren maintained a look of innocence until she said the last word. Then she laughed all over again.

Amber put on her best "get-over-it" expression. "I think we'll be fine. And could we not mention this to anyone else, *please?*"

Amber received no promises about silence, but she did get five firm hugs before she started home.

Amber took a long, hot shower before she got ready for bed. It was her fourth shower for the day if you counted the big water fight. She felt like she needed to just wash away all of the difficulties of the last week. She didn't even care when Ryan yelled at the bathroom door, "Leave some hot water for me, would ya?"

Afterward, she dried her hair a bit and then put on her favorite pajamas. She settled in at her desk to log on for a good-night chat. She turned the computer on, but nothing happened. Grinning, she reached down and held the plug in her hands. *Funny,* she thought, *the things you believe when you're afraid. I trusted this plug to keep me safe more than I trusted God to do that.*

She clicked on TodaysGirls.com in her Favorite Places list. Before she could enter the chat room, a familiar dialogue box popped up on the screen.

Don't depend on your own understanding.
Why do we think we know so much when we have so much to learn? We try to figure life out, but God is the only one who understands it all. Trust him when life is not fair and things are not going your way. Tough teacher? Bad friend? Family problems? He'll know what to do.

Amber thought about the reporter at the pool. *My understanding is certainly nothing to be depended on. Poor guy was just trying to help, and I thought he was a villain.*

When she signed on in the chat room, only three names were listed: nycbutterfly, chicChick, and rembrandt.

faithful1: Where is everybody?

nycbutterfly: Jellybean can't sign on with me already in. We don't have the second computer hooked up yet. She's here reading along tho. (hi, she says)

chicChick: I'm here, but I'm painting my toenails 2 so don't ask any quick questions.

rembrandt: we're all here.

faithful1: No, there's one missing.

nycbutterfly: what r u talking about?

rembrandt: <shocked and amazed> o no, u didn't!

chicChick: didn't what? didn't what?

newkid enters the room

faithful1: Hi there, newkid, glad you could make it.

newkid: thanks. Glad to be here. Cool site.

nycbutterfly: is newkid who I think she is?

chicChick: ???

rembrandt: Alex?

faithful1: it only seemed right. If she was smart enough to be the Stranger, I think she's smart enough to be a friend. Besides I figured HER TIME HAD COME. (ha!)

nycbutterfly: Ugh. Don't remind me again. OK, welcome, newkid. (jellybean says, yay!)

chicChick: I guess this means SHE'S GETTING HERS. LOL. Come on in girl.

rembrandt: u better be on your best behavior, new. By now u know that we have our own ways of dealing with things.

newkid: I got it--and they leave me freezing!

nycbutterfly: who picked your name?

faithful1: I did. It was something between 'newkid' and 'stranger_no_more' which was way too long.

newkid: I like it.

rembrandt: me too

faithful1: so it's official. We're a six-girl site and not a stranger online.

Net Ready, Set, Go!

I hope my words and thoughts please you.
Psalm 19:14

The characters of TodaysGirls.com chat online in the safest—and maybe most fun—of all chat rooms! They've created their own private Web site and room! Many Christian teen sites allow you to create your own private chat rooms, and there are other safe options.

Work with your parents to develop a list of safe, appropriate chat rooms. Earn Internet freedom by showing them you can make the right choices. *Honor your father and your mother. . . Deuteronomy 5:16*

Before entering a chat room, you'll select a user name. Although you can use your real name, a nickname is safer. Most people choose one that says something about who they are, like Amber's name, faithful1. Don't be discouraged if the name you select is already taken. You can use a similar one by adding a number at its end.

No one will notice your grammar in a chat room. Don't worry if you spell something wrong or forget to capitalize. Some people even misspell words on purpose. You might see a sentence like How R U?

But sometimes it's important to be accurate. Web site and e-mail addresses must be exact. Pay close attention to whether letters are upper or lowercase. Remember that Web site addresses don't use some punctuation marks, such as hyphens and apostrophes. (That's why the "Today's" in TodaysGirls.com has no apostrophe!) And instead of spaces between words, underlines are used to_make_a_space. And sometimes words just run together like onebigword.

Stranger Online

When you're in a chat room, remember real people are typing the words that appear on your screen. Treat them with the same respect you expect from them. Don't say anything you wouldn't want repeated in Sunday school. *Do for other people what you want them to do for you. Luke 6:31*

Sometimes people say mean, hurtful things—things that make us angry. This can happen in chat rooms too. In some chat rooms, you can highlight a rude person's name and click a button that says, "ignore," which will make his or her comments disappear from your screen. You always have the option to switch rooms or sign off. If a particular person becomes a continual problem, or if someone says something especially vicious, you should report this problem user to the chat service. *Ask God to bless those who say bad things to you. Pray for those who are cruel. . . . Luke 6:28-29*

Remember that Internet information is not always factual. Whether you're chatting or surfing Web sites, be skeptical about information and people. Not everything on the Internet is true. You don't have to be afraid of the Internet, but you should always be cautious. Practice caution with others even in Christian chat rooms.

It's okay to chat about your likes and dislikes, but *never* give out personal information. Do not tell anyone your name, phone number, address, or even the name of your school, team, church, or neighborhood. Be cautious. . . . *You will be like sheep among wolves. So be as smart as snakes. But also be like doves and do nothing wrong. Be careful of people. . . .Matthew 10:16-17*

STRANGER ONLINE

16/junior
e-name: faithful1
best friend: Maya
site area: Thought for the Day

Confident. Caring. Swimmer. Single-handedly built TodaysGirls.com Web site. Loves her folks. Big brother Ryan drives her nuts! Great friend. Got a problem? Go to Amber.

AMBE
THOMA:

JAMIE CHANDLER

PORTRAIT OF LIES

15/sophmore
e-name: rembrandt
best friend: Bren
site area: Artist's Corner

Quiet. Talented artist. Works at the Gnosh Pit after school. Dad left when she was little. Helps her mom with younger sisters Jordan and Jessica. Babysits for Coach Short's kids.

ALEX DIAZ

TANGLED WEB

14/freshman
e-name: newkid
best friend: Morgan
site area: to be determined . . .

Spicy. Hot-tempered Texan. Lives with grandparents because of parents' problems. Won state in freestyle swimming at her old school. Snoops. Into everything. Break the rules.

R U 4 REAL?

16/junior
e-name: nycbutterfly
best friend: Amber
site area: What's Hot—What's Not
(under construction)

MAYA CROSS

Fashion freak. Health nut. Grew up in New York City. Small town drives her crazy. Loves to dance. Dad owns the Gnosh Pit. Little sis Morgan is also a TodaysGirl.

BREN MICKLER

LUV@FIRST SITE

15/sophmore
e-name: chicChick
best friend: Jamie
site area: Smashin' Fashion

Funny. Popular. Outgoing. Spaz. Cheerleader. Always late. Only child. Wealthy family. Bren is chatting— about anything, online and off, except when she's eating junk food.

CHAT FREAK

14/freshman
e-name: jellybean
best friend: Alex
site area: Feeling All Write (under construction)

MORGAN
CROSS

The Web-ster. Spends too much time online. Overalls. M&Ms. Swim team. Tries to save the world. Close to her family—when her big sister isn't bossing her around.

Cyber Glossary

Bounced mail An e-mail that has been returned to its sender.

Chat A live conversation—typed or spoken through microphones—among individuals in a chat room.

Chat room A "place" on the Internet where individuals meet to "talk" with one another.

Crack To break a security code.

Download To receive information from a more powerful computer.

E-mail Electronic mail which is sent through the Internet.

E-mail address An Internet address where e-mail is received.

File Any document or image stored on a computer.

Floppy Disk A small, thin plastic object which stores information to be accessed by a computer.

Hacker Someone who tries to gain unauthorized access to another computer or network of computers.

Header Text at the beginning of an e-mail which identifies the sender, subject matter, and the time at which it was sent.

Homepage A Web site's first page.

Internet A worldwide electronic network that connects computers to each other.

Link Highlighted text or a graphic element which may be clicked with the mouse in order to "surf" to another Web site or page.

Log on/Log in To connect to a computer network.

Modem A device which enables computers to exchange information.

The Net The Internet.

Newbie A person who is learning or participating in something new.

Online To have Internet access. Can also mean to use the Internet.

Surf To move from page to page through links on the Web.

The Web The World Wide Web or WWW.

Upload To send information to a more powerful computer.